Bachelor.com

by

Kathye Quick

Bachelors Three Series

Bachelor.com

Cover Art by *Rae Monet, Inc. Design*

The Wild Rose Press, Inc.
PO Box 708
Adams Basin, NY 14410-0708
Visit us at www.thewildrosepress.com

Publishing History
First Sweetheart Rose Edition, 2015
Print ISBN 978-1-5092-0226-3
Digital ISBN 978-1-5092-0227-0

Bachelors Three Series
Published in the United States of America

Just as she had for the past three days, Kinley dumped the old flowers in the garbage can and filled the vase with fresh water from the sink in Jack's hospital bathroom. Off and on, Jack would open his eyes for a few minutes, making her jump up from the chair and lean over the bedrail so he could see her. A few times, she thought he tried to smile, but with everything he'd been through, she thought the action could just be the result of some sudden pain or gas that makes a newborn baby smile. The nurses assured her Jack would gradually become more alert, and she wanted to be there when he did. She put the flowers she bought into the vase and walked out of the bathroom.

"Hey."

She nearly dropped everything at the sound of Jack's voice. He had been lying so still when she came in she assumed he was still unconscious. "Hey yourself," she replied, fighting to keep her voice from breaking.

"I made you miss another dinner, didn't I?" His voice sounded like a strained whisper, and his eyes were open to only half-slits.

By sheer force of will, she controlled the forming tears. "I haven't been that hungry lately." She put the flowers on the bed tray and touched his hand, afraid to touch anything else. "Don't try to talk. I'm only staying a minute. You need your rest."

His finger lifted. "I can talk. Sort of. I'm shot so full of drugs that nothing hurts, though the bandages don't allow for much jaw movement."

She tried to smile, but failed.

"Don't look so scared, Kin. Everything got put back together. I just have to spend some time healing."

Praise for Kathye Quick

"Kathye Quick is an incredible author who writes with heart, style, and imagination. Her books will make you laugh or bring a tear to your eye, and will always keep you coming back for more."

~*Linda J. Parisi, Author of the Nobility Series*
~*~

"…fabled beauty and the beast story line brought to the modern world starring a high-powered businesswoman with an attraction for a techno-geek computer wizard who fails to see his own 'hunki-ness.' Snappy dialogue won me over immediately. The unlikely attraction ranked second as to why I couldn't stop turning the pages, wanting more and more and MORE!!! BACHELOR.COM is a winner in my book…"

~*Award-winning author Kat Henry Doran*
~*~

"Quick delivers an engaging twist on a classic tale as a high-powered career woman helps transform a nerdy programmer into a sexy hunk. Humor and emotion combine in a story that will keep you reading until you breathlessly reach the very last page."

~*Caridad Pineiro,*
NY Times and USA Today Bestselling Author
~*~

"Beauty and the Beast Tech style, that's what we have with Quick's BACHELOR.COM. Entertaining, lively, romantic and humorous love story that will have you wanting a second story about these two lovers."

~*Patt Mihailoff*
2009-2010 Author and Mentor of the Year RWA-NYC

Dedication

For Mom

Chapter One

Dakota pulled down the night vision glasses and scanned the area in front of him. A few minor obstacles stood between him and the target—some cars, shrubs, a fence—all colored green in the amplified light of the intensifier tube in the night vision glasses through which he peered. Nothing he couldn't handle. Waiting for the right moment to strike…well, that might be a bit harder.

Never one of his virtues, patience always sat in the middle of his chest like the tormenting weight of possible failure during a mission. How many had there been? Twenty? Thirty? He'd lost count. Each mission became more complicated than the one before, testing his reactions, his instincts, his training. While he hated the waiting, concentrating on the future always saved his sanity. Soon he'd reach Mission Chief, on his way to Commander, a rank yet unachieved by anyone.

He felt sweat drool down the back of his neck but ignored it. Focusing on the house, he inched his way forward on his stomach, his army-issued night camos skimming the combination of dirt and weeds like a gliding snake as he moved across the front lawn of the safe house in the run-down urban neighborhood.

A smile crossed his face. Safe house. Big mistaken assumption. No one could ever really be safe when JOLT came into play. The Joint Operations Liberation

Team got assigned when everything and everyone else had failed. JOLT never did. In order to keep the streak going, he had to either bring back the mark alive or make sure no one else could. Move in too soon, and he could get overrun; move in too late, he might miss his target. He would have to lay low and wait until just the right opportunity presented itself. He only hoped it would be soon. His trigger finger was getting mighty itchy.

Dakota didn't have much longer to wait. A flutter of the curtain on the back door made the decision for him. He bolted up the back stairs two at a time and kicked open the door. Whoever was in the room had gone. Then, angling his Beretta 92 to the left and to the right in sweeping lines with straight arms, he moved in, expecting to find the barrel of the gun of whoever moved the curtain trained on him at any time. Mildly surprised, he found the first few rooms clear. Slowly, he circled to the front of the house, gaze constantly scanning. A barely perceptible movement behind him kicked his instincts into action, and he spun. Dropping to one knee, he got off a perfect shot to the center of an attacking gunman's forehead, dropping him.

More men came in response to the gunfire, and Dakota picked off each with the precision that earned him the Red Dead designation—a highly prized term at JOLT. After a short barrage of bullets, the ensuing silence screamed in eerie contrast as he reloaded his magazine with twenty rounds. Then he stood, taking an offensive posture and looking down at the bodies at his feet, understanding the mission was not over by a long shot. His mark was conspicuously missing.

Stepping over the fallen, he moved to the staircase,

aiming at the top landing as he slowly began a silent climb. He could hear footsteps above and strained to make out the direction. He stepped from the top step to the hallway and listened. Silence. In sequence, he kicked open each door on the second floor, checking for anyone inside, until only one door remained.

Pressing his body against the wall, elbows in, gun firmly in hand, he took a deep breath. Then, spinning, he booted open the final door and came face to face with his mark just as blackness fell.

****

Kinley Adams stepped in front of the flat screen TV on the living room wall. A second later, a computer-generated voice announced. "Mission Failure. Game over. Five lives remaining."

"You just got me killed," Jack Reeves, aka Dakota in the latest video game he had been developing, said.

"Never underestimate a woman scorned," Kinley responded. "You promised me dinner."

Jack set the controller on the floor and looked at his watch. "Sorry, Kin, the time got away from me. War Zone III is supposed to go to marketing in two weeks and there are still some kinks I need to work out."

"There will be kinks in my stomach soon. I waited at the restaurant for over two hours." She felt both anger and disappointment build. She thought she had gotten used to the way he immersed himself in his work and ended up late for everything, but today, she had something special planned. Today, no excuse would be acceptable.

Jack grimaced. "Why do you put up with me anyway?"

"My brother thinks you're a rock star because you

3

design computer games for a living."

"That's all?"

She rolled her eyes. "On an empty stomach, that's all you're getting."

"Just give me one more second. I almost know what's wrong." He picked up an extra controller and held it out. "But I need your help to test out the theory."

Kinley exhaled, grabbed the joystick, and plopped down on the couch next to him. "Okay, but this time I'm designing my own avatar."

"You don't like the one I made?" Jack tabbed over to the character list on the video game and brought up a curvy red-headed game player named Cinnamon. In an instant, a sexy woman—clad in tight black leather, gun in hand, ammo belt around a slender waist—revolved in the center of the TV screen.

Kinley looked at the hot babe center screen and cut her gaze sideways. "I do not look anything like that." She glanced back at the screen. "And if you ask me, she's had some work done." She looked at the flawless body on the screen and shook her head. Was this Jack's perfect woman? "People like that do not exist in the real world."

"And that's part of the fun. Take Dakota." Tall and toned with an athlete's build and a soldier's muscles, Jack's character stood next to Kinley's on the TV screen.

"Hmmm. Looks like he works out."

"You never mentioned being attracted to muscle-bound guys."

"They have their place."

Jack laughed. "And where would that place be?"

"Out somewhere, saving the world for democracy."

She cocked her head. "And you never mentioned you like redheaded bombshells who look like they belong in *Penthouse Magazine*."

"They have their place," he mimicked.

"I know I'll be sorry, but where would that place be?"

"With guys like Dakota, not guys like me."

Kinley thought she heard a pang of regret in his voice. She pointed to the TV screen. "Is that who you want to be, Jack?"

"I did. When I was a teenager. I even bought a set of weights with my summer job money. Pumped iron for a month straight and thought I could see a bicep muscle. But come September and school, things went right back to being the way nature intended. Jocks versus Geeks. Teeny bicep muscle or not, I knew my place was last in line and last to be picked in gym class."

"So, you worked out your brain instead of your body, went to Harvard, got your Bachelor's and your Master's, and are now on your way to computer game design heaven with the goal of having those jocks work in your stock room someday."

He laughed. "Something like that."

"Something like that or exactly like that?"

"Having all the guys who ever gave me a purple nurple or wedgie work for me would be a small measure of revenge for all the grief I put up with just to be left alone." His smile faded. "When I went through that awkward stage, which for me lasted until I was twenty-two, I often wondered what being one of the beautiful people would have been like."

"But you are," Kinley corrected.

His smile came back. "You're a good friend, Kinley, but you don't have to coddle. I'm comfortable in my nerd-skin."

"Good." She took the game controller from his hand. "Because the world needs guys like you to stay in balance." She smiled. "Dakota there probably can't even set a DVR, and you haven't met a motherboard you can't improve upon." She rocked her hand in the air. "Balance is a beautiful thing."

"I'm happy in my niche. Besides, not everyone likes spending eight hours a day in a gym trying to turn his abs into the proverbial six-pack." He looked down at his waistline and patted his stomach. "Working on these babies to even be a one-pack could take years."

She walked to the flat screen TV hanging on the wall and studied her alter ego for a moment. Then she spun to face him. "Oh, Cinnamon here might just like the brainiac type, considering her profession as a ruthless mercenary. I bet guys who could make a radio from a paperclip, some aluminum foil, and gum would do quite well with her."

"Only until her real boyfriend, the man she had sworn to protect, and just happens to be the President-elect of the United States who, coincidently, also looks like a GQ model, took her in his arms, and declared the mission a success. We sidekicks are then relegated to the background while the credits roll around their kiss."

She read the look on his face easily. He looked positively crushed. "That isn't the way I would have the movie end."

He shrugged his answer. "Let's face it, Kin, in a perfectly balanced world, we not-so-perfect people know our place. The first Rule of Attraction has been drummed into our heads head since we got our first pair of horn rims at age ten—girls don't make passes at guys in glasses."

"That's not true," she countered.

Jack captured her gaze. "You never have."

The serious tone of his voice hit her like an F5 tornado, driving everything she knew she should say into the stratosphere. "Jack, I…"

"It's okay, Kin." He shut down the video game and stood. "It's nature's plan."

Everything she should have said came rushing back at once. Why didn't she tell him that she thought he was perfect when she had the chance? Now it was too late. Argue the point, and her words would sound like a pity-pass. Agree with him, and the gap between them grew bigger. The only way to salvage the moment was to verbally tap-dance around the point. For now.

"We'll talk about this later, but Cinnamon and I are not hunting down the bad guys with you, or anyone for that matter, until we get something to eat."

Jack smiled and stood, digging in the pocket of his jeans for his car keys. "How about something from A Taste of the Dragon?" He held them up and waggled his eyebrows. "*Kung pao* chicken? You order, I'll go get it."

Kinley looked him up and down. "You're going out like that?"

Jack's brow furrowed. "Like what?" he asked.

"You're wearing the same clothes you had on when I left here last night." She walked to him and adjusted his black glasses. "And you need to get those fixed. The electrical tape wrapped around the earpiece is about to let loose." She cocked her head. "Ever think about getting vision-correcting laser surgery for those brown eyes of yours?"

Jack squeezed the black wad holding his glasses together. "I don't trust stuff like that. Too technical for me."

"Technical? You thrive on technical." She pointed to the cartridge in the game box. "You live for technical."

"Not when it comes to my body. For that I just trust chicken soup and aspirin."

"Jack, Jack, Jack."

"Kinley, Kinley, Kinley."

She smiled. "You need a make-over. Really."

"I fix video games for a living. All I need is the internet."

"We're going shopping tomorrow."

"Why?"

"Dinner party in three weeks," she reminded him.

Jack looked positively horrified. "With shoes?"

"And socks. No flip-flops."

"And after that?"

"You can go back to being the couch potato that I love."

Jack's smile started to grow before she finished the sentence. "You love me?"

"If you really want to know, you'll feed me." She pulled out her cell, but didn't dial. "Unless you'd rather be helping an unrealistically physical female redheaded avatar beat up on some bad guys in a burned-out city somewhere in Asia."

He shook his head. "Not this time. Order."

****

An hour later, Kinley's stomach rumbled louder.

Jack still wasn't back with the food, and she needed sustenance. Being a project manager in the planning division for Excalibur Retail Development normally came with perks like traveling around the country checking development sites, but today, the workday had been lousy. The air conditioning didn't work, all five planners she assigned to the latest improvement project made requests at the same time, and the engineers were equally demanding. With the redesign of the new shopping and sports complex due before the city planning board in just short of a month, she had to skip lunch and work overtime. Her wrinkled suit jacket lay across a chair, and her blouse, more than a bit wet in all the wrong places, still stuck to her back.

Stomach sending out the music of starvation, she stood in front of the air conditioner that rested precariously in the only window in Jack's living room. The outdated unit wheezed like a four-pack-a-day smoker, but at least it worked. For now. She'd have to get after Jack to replace it. After all, this was New Jersey in the summer, ninety-plus degrees with enough humidity to melt the polar icecap. Nothing like it anywhere else in the nation. But she didn't want to be anywhere else. Especially since Jack swooped into her life like the action heroes he created and saved her computer from certain doom at the hands of the latest predatory virus. After the fix, she promised to stick to the keys she knew how to use and let him take care of the rest. Among those keyboard controls and the "on" and "off" switches, she came to realize she had somehow fallen in love with Jack along the way. To her, he was perfect. She would just have to convince him of that fact.

A growl from her stomach reminded her. Where was he anyway?

She looked out the window over the air conditioner and saw Maria Falucci, Jack's closest neighbor, hurrying up the driveway. She opened the door just as the older woman got up to the porch. "Hello, Maria."

"Mr. Jack," Maria said in her Italian-accented English. Breathless, she held up her forefinger and took some deep breaths to calm herself.

"Jack's not here. He went out to get take-out for dinner. He should be back any minute."

Maria huffed and puffed as she caught her breath. "No, he won't. I come-a over as fast as I could."

Her accent suddenly sounded heavier than usual. The feeling one gets when something bad is about to happen grew inside Kinley. "What's wrong?" She looked past Maria into the empty street.

"Mr. Jack in big accident."

Kinley felt her heart clench. "What do you mean?"

"Joey, my husband, he was at the store and see Mr. Jack's car pushed up against the concrete divider in the road. Mr. Jack go to the hospital in *ambulanza*. He say the lights and sirens were on and they drove *molto velocemente*...very fast."

Kinley barely heard the rest of the details as a white noise took over inside her brain. Maria explained a delivery truck ran a red light at the intersection and hit Jack's car as he pulled out of the strip mall. As the white noise in her head grew louder, she heard words not sentences. Three cars. Jack's crushed. Jaws of Life. A jolting few minutes passed until her brain registered that something terrible had really happened to Jack. "Which hospital, Maria?" she choked out.

"The Medical Center. The closest."

"Do you know how he is?"

"I try to call, but they only talk to *familia*. I come-a as fast as I can when I hear."

Kinley grabbed her purse and headed for the driveway. "Thank you, Maria." She yanked open the car door and jumped in.

"You call and tell me how he is," Maria shouted after her. "If there's something the neighbors can do, you tell me. Mr. Jack is good man, *uomo meraviglioso*. Okay?"

"Okay," Kinley called back with a wave out the car window. She hit the Bluetooth button on the steering wheel and called the hospital at the same time as she fishtailed the car out of the driveway. While she waited for someone to answer, she felt her heart squeeze tight at the thought of Jack hurt.

She met him two years earlier when her brother called the Nerd Herd, the techno-troubleshooting business recommended in the instruction booklet for the new video game he'd just blown up. Jack showed up and began tinkering with the gaming system about the same time she pressed "yes" to the question on her computer: Do *you want to permanently delete the selected files?* Why she pressed the button, she still didn't know, but the blood-curdling scream she let out when she realized the company's third-quarter report now resided in the cyber dump brought Jack running. She sobbed like a damn fool while he clicked, typed, and double-clicked the files back into existence, doling out tissues while she sniffled, like drying tears was a normal part of his day.

After an hour or so, not only had he fixed her

brother's game, he'd also fixed her desktop and laptop and set up controls even she couldn't screw up to protect her data. He spent another hour showing her how not to lose her Power Point presentations, and a few more minutes talking her out of her phone number. After that, he became a part of her life. She couldn't lose him now.

Finally, someone at the hospital answered.

"Hello, I'm inquiring about a patient just brought in within the hour. Jack Reeves." She waited. "An accident. He was in a car accident." She nearly choked on the words. "Yes, I'm his sister." She crossed her fingers with the lie, hoping the gesture would make it right. "I just heard about it." Thankfully, Maria told her the hospital would only talk to relatives. Knowing the rules ahead of time made the lie slip out a lot smoother.

The fib seemed to work, or at least got her transferred somewhere deeper inside the hospital. The wait between answering voices felt like an eternity as the call moved from floor to floor, but that also gave her some hope. Apparently, he wasn't isolated in ICU, so then maybe he wasn't too badly hurt.

"Ms. Reeves?"

She almost didn't answer, but then remembered who she claimed to be. "Yes?" She listened to someone tell her that Jack was still in surgery and his condition was labeled "serious." He needed more testing and possibly more surgery when his medical status improved. But the voice on the line couldn't tell her what his injuries were, or when he'd be taken to his room and cleared for visitors. A litany of hospital rules came next as if being read from a card. She listened politely and hung up.

Right now, she didn't care about hospital rules. She didn't care about anyone's rules. Jack had always been there for her and now he needed payback. She pitied anyone who tried to stop her from seeing him. By the time she parked and sprinted for the doors, a potential problem surfaced. She was supposed to be Jack's sister. She hoped the person in charge would believe her.

True, some siblings didn't always look alike, but she and Jack could not be more dissimilar. He was over six feet and she climbed to a whopping five foot four…in heels. He didn't believe in working out and she ran two miles every day. She had blond hair and blue eyes. People told her that she was cute, like a young Reese Witherspoon. His dark hair, chopped short like he cut it himself, underscored the fact he didn't care much about how he looked. Outdated black-rimmed glasses covered his brown eyes and he liked old, comfortable clothes—very unlike her stylish designer suits.

Still, when she asked at the desk, no one challenged her claim to be a relative. Possibly because she looked so wilted from the heat. Who would go out like that unless they had to? But, at the moment, she didn't care what she looked like. All she cared about was getting to Jack and finding out how he was.

Questions and directions led her to the Three East waiting room. The long hall of cloned rooms was not a specialty wing. She felt the tension in her neck and shoulders release a little. Maybe he had only been tossed around a little, and she could bring him home.

****

Light from the morning sunrise filtered in through the blinds in the waiting room about the same time

Kinley decided she could not stand sitting there a moment longer. She walked to the nurses' station. "I know you told me you'd let me know as soon as"—she hesitated, getting the words right—"my brother was in his room, but..." The horrible thoughts accompanying the uncertain preposition chocked off her voice.

"I was just coming to get you, Ms. Reeves," the dark haired nurse said. "He just came down from recovery and is in 387." She pointed. "End of the hall, hang a right."

Her hurried footsteps echoed on the tile floor and her mind whirled with the words, *he will be okay, he will be okay.* But her heart jerked when she poked her head into his room. The occupant in the bed by the window was far from looking okay. He looked a lot worse than someone who had been just tossed around a little.

Covered by a sheet, the man in the bed looked like a mummy. Bandages completely encased his face except for a narrow slit across his eyes, and another opening that freed his mouth and nose. A metal hinge trapped his neck and jaw, and his right arm, immobilized by a sling, sat on a pillow on his chest. A cast encased his right leg, which hung from a contraption attached to the bed. Tubes connected him to beeping and clicking machines.

She tiptoed in, feeling like her heart was in her throat, and a dozen memories of Jack flashed through her mind. Like a movie playing, she could see him walking around his kitchen, glasses askew, in jeans and T-shirts, flip-flops or no shoes at all, looking like the stereotypical computer geek. His scruffy appearance, and his house a few boxes away from a feature on that reality TV show about hoarding, meant mistaken opinions might come easily, but the neighbors knew better. They camped out on his doorstep when they blew up the hard drives in their computer or when they had other tangible problems they couldn't begin to solve—from broken fences to broken dreams. Jack was one of those people who never said no to anyone. He stepped up and took charge.

Looking at his white-bandaged face now made her really angry. She wanted to scream at whoever did this. *You almost killed him.* The words raced through her mind, tripping all the fear sensors, sending her heart into race mode. Over the last two years, she never thought much about him not being there until this very moment. The thought scared her to death. The reason she didn't want to lose him wasn't because he treated her with respect and made her comfortable whenever they were together, unlike some of the guys she dated who made her feel like dessert. And certainly it wasn't because he could fix whatever she could break on anything electronic. She simply realized, and partly because of this accident, this terrible accident, the time had come to tell Jack that she loved him. Time was precious, and she needed him to know exactly how she felt. Even if he didn't believe her or feel the same way.

****

Just as she had for the past three days, Kinley dumped the old flowers in the garbage can and filled the vase with fresh water from the sink in Jack's hospital bathroom. Off and on, Jack would open his eyes for a few minutes, making her jump up from the chair and lean over the bedrail so he could see her. A few times, she thought he tried to smile, but with everything he'd been through, she thought the action could just be the result of some sudden pain or gas that makes a newborn baby smile. The nurses assured her Jack would gradually become more alert, and she wanted to be there when he did. She put the flowers she bought into the vase and walked out of the bathroom.

"Hey."

She nearly dropped everything at the sound of Jack's voice. He had been lying so still when she came in she assumed he was still unconscious. "Hey yourself," she replied, fighting to keep her voice from breaking.

"I made you miss another dinner, didn't I?" His voice sounded like a strained whisper, and his eyes were open to only half-slits.

By sheer force of will, she controlled the forming tears. "I haven't been that hungry lately." She put the flowers on the bed tray and touched his hand, afraid to touch anything else. "Don't try to talk. I'm only staying a minute. You need your rest."

His finger lifted. "I can talk. Sort of. I'm shot so full of drugs that nothing hurts, though the bandages don't allow for much jaw movement."

She tried to smile, but failed.

"Don't look so scared, Kin. Everything got put back together. I just have to spend some time healing."

She widened her eyes, her heart pounding. "What came apart?"

"My face," he whispered back. "My arm and my leg, for sure. And I got a brand new knee."

"Your arm looks awful." She hoped to keep the tone light, but her voice sounded more like a choked whisper, thanks to the sight of all the tubes and wires coming from his body.

"I must have tried to protect my face with my arms when the car hit. I'm pretty sure I look like hell from the reaction of every doctor and nurse who looked at me."

She made herself smile, not wanting him to know how frightening he did look. "Shh. Don't try to talk any more. I'm not staying long."

He motioned to the bandages on his face. "Stay. Nothing hurts. Really. I'm dosed up with morphine."

"You sure you want me here?"

"Yes. What about your dinner, though?"

"Forget dinner," Kinley said quickly. "I had something from the vending machines."

"I can only promise something like milk shakes and ice cream anyway. For a while, I'll be using a straw to eat."

She bit down on her lip, fresh tears forming in her eyes. "I'll take it."

"Hey, don't look so upset. Everything will work again."

"You aren't one of your video game characters, Jack. You only come with one life."

"I'll be fine," he assured.

"You better be."

"Besides, you know how much I like working from home."

"Heck of a way to make sure you do," Kinley replied, untangling the call bell cord near his hand.

"I like being casual."

"That is a definite understatement. Are they giving you enough joy juice?" she asked him, suddenly wanting to make sure he really didn't hurt.

"Too much, because I feel kinda good, and I don't think I'm supposed to."

She smiled. Even with the strained sound of his voice, she could hear the hint of his humor. "I want to know what happened, but I'm still not convinced you should talk much," she told him. "That contraption around your jaw looks medieval."

"But nothing hurts too much," he assured her. "My jaw is sore, and I can't open my mouth very much, so something happened there. I was really out of it when I got here. I don't really know what anyone did to me in the ER. I know I've been in and out of surgery a few times, but what they did to me in there, I have no idea either."

Kinley grabbed a chair and set it as close to the bed as possible. "You really made a mess of yourself. Lots of broken stuff here." She scanned down his sheet-covered body. "Leg, too. And you already told me you have a new knee."

"A couple of doctors are coming back later tonight to let me know exactly what else is new. Ah, Kin?"

His sudden hesitation made her lean forward, alarm stiffening her muscles. "What? What's wrong? Do I need to call someone?"

"No. But I have to tell you this. You may not recognize me when the bandages come off. A plastic surgeon came in right before you. He said I hit the windshield, and told me straight out that I needed my face rebuilt almost from scratch." He chuckled. "Guess my days as a handsome hunk are over."

Kinley felt as though a fist clamped around her heart. She knew he was waiting for her to say something, and she wanted to say the right thing. She just didn't know what it should be. Though the bandages concealed his expression, she could feel his gaze searching hers face. She knew he was joking about the handsome hunk thing. Jack was an average Joe, a fade-into-the-woodwork guy who didn't care about fashion. He worked fixing computer games. Complete with dated haircut, a few extra pounds around the middle, and no desire to even pick up *GQ,* he was comfortable in his own skin. Looks didn't matter to him, and she never really thought about his physical appearance either. He had won her over with his personality and smile.

But from what he had just said, he seemed concerned about how he might look now. Though Jack didn't have a vain bone in his body, she could tell the thought of facing a drastic change in the way he looked unnerved him. She vowed to step up and give him the support he needed so he could cope with any changes or scars once the bandages came off.

She reached for his hand and tangled her fingers with his. "Well heck, maybe we could pick out a face we both like then."

"Now, there's a thought."

She smiled. "But then again, I don't really feel like fending off a whole lot of women who may be chasing you once your Adonis face becomes public. Maybe I'll ask the doctor to leave a few scars."

"But don't chicks love scars? I heard that in that Keanu Reeves movie you like so much."

"You're right." Kinley tapped her chin with her forefinger. "They do appeal to a woman's bad boy fantasy." She waggled her head back and forth, studying at the bandages on his face. "This could be a problem."

"The problem is, I have no idea why I waited until age thirty-three to find out women had bad boy fantasies. While I recover, I may explore that a bit more. What if I get a tattoo?"

"No, you don't. Women's fantasies are on a need-to-know basis and the only thing you need to know right now is when you're going home."

"But I'm getting a whole new face. Now, we'll both be cute."

Kinley narrowed her eyes. "Sounds like you're feeling better."

"Maybe I am, but I probably should wait until the happy juice wears off to find out for sure."

She heard approaching footsteps and looked toward the door. "I'm worried any second now someone will be in here to kick me out and take you for another test or something. So, let's cut to the end. What do you need?"

"Call Rashesh and tell him I won't be finishing the video game on time. He'll have to push back production for a few weeks. Then…"

She pressed a finger to her lips and cut him off with a loud, "Shh. Work, no; heal, yes."

Rashesh Patel was the CEO of the company that produced the video game Jack was working on the day of the accident. She knew War Zone III was being heavily promoted by *Gaming Magazine* as the next big thing. She also hoped the game would be Jack's ticket out of the Help Department and into Product Development.

"But, Kinley, Rashesh…"

Her forefinger now gently lay across his lips.

"Rashesh can write the code for a few weeks while you get better. We have more important things to do. Like what about your parents? Shall I call them?"

"No," Jack said quickly. "I don't want to worry them. I'll be fine. Broken arms and legs will heal, but this face-thing is starting to really annoy me. I'll talk to them when I have some answers for the questions Mom will surely ask."

She saw his eyes close as though he suddenly couldn't fight off sleep. "Listen, I'm outta here. You need to rest."

"It's the drugs," he protested. "I just zone out every now and then."

"Liar." She stood, but still held onto his hand. "I'm out of here, but I'll be back tomorrow with some things you'll need. I assume you'll want your toothbrush, and you'll probably want some pajamas."

"Umm, I don't do pajamas."

"Oh." She could feel a flush blooming on her cheeks. "I didn't know you slept commando."

"Despite all my efforts to the contrary."

To Kinley, the comment sounded more like a comment rather than an attempt at humor. The flush deepened. "Well, with all the gauze on your face, you probably won't need a razor. I'll bring some books and magazines. And I'll do it all before I go to work in the morning. Getting up at 5:00 a.m. isn't something I'd even do for my beloved Keanu, so this is a true test of how much I love you."

"That's the second time you said you loved me. If you aren't careful, I could believe it."

Their fingers had been loosely twined, but now his hand clutched hers as his grip tightened. "As much as

21

one friend loves another," she quickly explained. Or had she quickly lied? She'd answer that question as soon as Jack was better and could actually concentrate. She smiled. "Now, is there anything else you think you might need?"

"No."

He sounded disappointed. She had upset him. That wouldn't help the healing process one bit. She'd better leave before she said something else wrong. Her feelings could wait. His recovery couldn't. "Make a mental list if you do think of something, and I'll pick it up in the morning." She felt his hand loosen.

"Thanks for coming, Kin."

"Not a problem." But when she tried to head for the door, she couldn't just leave him. He looked so alone, so lost. In the hall outside his door, carts rolled by and nurses called out, while the loudspeaker kept snapping out codes, adding to the sterile surroundings. She couldn't walk away without doing something to let him know how much he did matter.

So she bent down to find a spot to kiss him, but instead found a most complicated challenge. His face and brow and most of his head were wrapped in gauze. The only uncovered part of him was his mouth. With a smile, she covered his lips with hers in a light kiss so she wouldn't hurt him.

But on contact, her pulse bucked and then bolted to a fast, steady rate. His lips felt soft and warm, and though lighter than a soft touch of silk, the kiss could have been a crush of passion for the way her heart reacted. *Interesting. Interesting and nice.* But even as the warmth continued, the feeling soon gave way to a cold burst of panic.

What if he noticed?

What if he didn't?

Suddenly, she couldn't decide which would bother her more.

She straightened, breaking the contact, and forced her voice to be calm. "Okay. I'm outta here. You behave and go right to sleep. No chasing the help around in the halls and no wild parties at the nurses' station while I'm gone." Then she bolted for the door.

She made it outside of his room and out of his sight before releasing her smile. What in the world had come over her? Jack could have been killed. The thought scared the heck out of her. Seeing him in bandages with tubes all over had driven home that terrible point and, despite the seriousness of his condition, she felt her hormones doing the strangest things.

She shrugged off the building notion that change was coming and she could do nothing about it, and zoned in on practicality. Without talking to a doctor, she had no idea what Jack's prognosis might be or what he would face in the weeks ahead. The only thing she did know for sure was whatever would come, whatever he needed, she would be more than willing to tackle as long as Jack got well.

Chapter Two

"How is my favorite mummy doing today? Roaming the halls scaring the nurses? Trying to fix every computer glitch in the place?" Kinley asked when she entered Jack's hospital room.

Jack's pulse stopped and then raced faster than a runaway train. For the past month, Kinley had come in at the same time every day. Last night, she had told him she wouldn't be in so early. Because he didn't expect her, he had no time to mentally prepare. Now the sound of her voice made his heart dip into that wild well of forbidden water.

But only because he was hopelessly in love with her. He always considered her the princess to his frog, the beauty to his beast. She oozed style, and he could be a cast member in *What Not to Wear*. If that had been the only problem, he might have held onto the fantasy that maybe someday he could convince her to give him a shot. But now? After all this? The chance might be gone forever. He didn't want her pity; he wanted her heart. A situation like the nerd and the beauty queen scenario would be easy. His situation was far worse than that.

Being cooped up in a tediously monotonous hospital for the last few weeks had given him far too much time to think. All he could think about was what he would do if Kinley ever discovered the real truth before he could tell her. He had meant to do it many times. Even that fateful night. He'd made a reservation at her favorite restaurant, arranged to have flowers delivered to the table, and asked the maître'd to make sure they weren't disturbed. But he got caught up in the video game and missed the moment. Then the accident happened, and all Kinley's attention focused on him. Selfishly, he liked it. Recklessly, he put off saying anything about his other life. Now, like the coward he was, he felt afraid to tell her, afraid things would change once he did.

He moved the bed to more of a sitting up position, watching as Kinley took off her jacket, revealing a slim suit that showed off her figure. Not in a flashy sort of way, but just enough to be a feast for his eyes. The black skirt palmed the curve of her fanny, and the short red jacket revealed enough of her neckline to show off the castle pendant she always wore. Her blond hair was stylishly shaggy, the way he liked it best, as though he had run his fingers through it during a kiss. The style framed a perfect face with big blue eyes. He smiled, thinking of how she hated to be called cute, but she certainly was. Cute. Pert. Darling. Irresistible. Words he never used on any other woman, but used on her endlessly in the privacy of his own mind.

The metal hospital chair scraped along the floor with a noisy screech, jarring him out of his reverie.

Kinley pulled it close to the bed and sat. "Am I right about the tech support part at least?"

"The hospital mainframe could use some big time updating and the database is ancient. I promised I'd give the IT Department an once-over when I got out of here," he told her. "I thought you weren't coming today."

"Couldn't stay away. You know how much I love horror films. Vampires and werewolves are getting overdone, but mummies? They're kind of like a present to unwrap."

He laughed, but stopped short of telling her the pleasure would be his to let her.

"Any fresh torture today?"

"No. I'm good."

Gently, she reached out and touched the bandage across his cheek. "Any pain?"

Only when I think about you leaving me. "None."

"You always say that. And while I think those white bandages are sexy and everything, I am getting awfully sick and tired of not seeing your face. I can't tell if you're happy, sad, hurting, or hungry. Before, I could always tell what you were thinking by the expression on your face, especially whether or not you were lying."

No, you couldn't. I've been living a lie for the past two years. "I'm almost at the end of this."

"I talked to the plastic surgeon a few minutes ago. He still thinks I'm your sister so he didn't hesitate to give me details." She leaned forward in the chair. "I know you must be feeling really raw, but the next surgery you have will be the last time he plans on cutting into your face. So once you heal from that one, you're home free."

"Yes, and home to real food. If someone offered me a steak or a million dollars right now, I'd take the steak. This liquid diet really stinks."

He saw her eyes swim with sympathy.

"The broken jaw was the biggest problem but

you're on the mend now. Not much longer. The first home-cooked meal is on me." She shot him a mega-watt grin. "Just think about it. A new face isn't the only thing you're getting. You must have lost those love handles you used to have, because when I hug you, there's less of what used to be there. When you get out, you and I are going on a super shopping trip for all the new clothes you'll need."

"Sweat pants have elastic waistbands and T-shirts aren't form fitting. I'll be okay."

"New face, new body, new look. It's a woman's dream."

"And a man's nightmare."

Kinley stood and perched a hip on the bed. "Let's discuss that dream a little later. Just for fun. I'd like a shot at making over a new Jack Reeves."

"I thought *Extreme Makeover* only does houses."

She tossed her head. "You're not quite that bad. A little *What Not to Wear* is more like it. With all you're going through, getting a new face, you deserve to get a little style too."

"You may be disappointed, Kin. The doctor told me he wouldn't do more than was necessary, so I probably won't look all that different." A feeling of dread spread inside. He knew he would probably not look the same as he did before, but he didn't want to think about any changes right now.

He saw a playful look come into her eyes.

"Can I place an order?"

"For?"

Her fingertips traced the padded bandage. "Johnny Depp's nose." Her finger moved to his chin. "Brad Pitt's jawline."

Even through the thick bandages, he felt her gently cup his cheek.

"Cheekbones like Alex O'Laughlin's but with the dimples of Mario Lopez."

"With all that cutting and pasting, you'd better throw in the scars of Victor Frankenstein."

She grimaced. "There's always that."

Jack started to laugh. "Ow."

"What's wrong? Should I call the nurse?"

"No. My ribs kill me when I laugh." Plus, his broken arm itched. The bandages restricted his sight and movement, and his face hurt in general from all the cutting and hammering the plastic surgeon had done. But Kinley smiled, and he could forget it all when he saw that. "But it's okay. Laughter is the best medicine, so they say."

"Do they also say when all the torture of physical therapy will be over?"

"The hard part is already done. All that's left is outpatient therapy twice a week." He shifted in the bed, and his whole body hurt, but he wouldn't let her know that. Instead, he pointed to the hallway. "Tell me about life outside that door. Did they cure cancer or find life on the moon while I've been here?"

"Nothing that drastic."

While he listened to her update him on the status of the world he left, Jack let his mind run back to the day they met. She was full of sass now, but that day she'd gotten his attention by almost throwing her laptop across the room. He barely grabbed it out of her hand as her arm flew forward. He made her promise not to touch it while he fixed her little brother's video problems. When he got back, she was staring at the computer like something would burst forth and take a bite out of her neck. Over the next hour, she followed him around like she was his shadow, looking over his shoulder and asking all sorts of questions.

A few times, he grabbed her hand right before she tried to "help" by pressing one key or another. Finally, he had to pick her up and deposit her on a chair across the room. He drew an imaginary line in the rug with his foot and told her if she tried to cross it, she would be transported to another dimension by code running inside the operating system. He knew she didn't really believe him, but she stayed put long enough for him to finish undoing what she'd done and then back up the files on an external hard drive in case she ever did it again.

After a few mouse clicks to set the automatic backup and maintenance programs, he turned to face her with every intention of leaving, and found that he couldn't. That instant, something happened that never happened before. His heart did the slam-dunk thing, his hormones ran all out like a broken faucet, and his nerves tried to electrocute him with high-voltage lightning bolts.

Of course, she wasn't for him. He recognized that fact right away. Kinley was an attractive woman, and he was, for all intents and purposes, the consummate nerd. The robot voice inside his head rose almost immediately. *Warning, warning, warning, Jack Reeves.*

Look what happened when King Kong wanted the blond. When Romeo messed around with a Capulet. Heck, Lancelot and Guinevere were responsible for ruining a perfectly good medieval myth. When a guy acted on what he was feeling for a woman way out of his league, nothing ever followed but gut-wrenching pain and heartbreak. After all, there was love, and there was *love*. A man had to recognize which one he had. If he found he had the wrong one, he just bit the bullet and was grateful for the one he got.

"You haven't heard one word I even said."

Kinley, the vulnerable, fragile flower he was sure he had fallen in love with, spoke with the exasperation and tone of a perfect commando. He turned to her and smiled.

"I came all the way here to perk up your day, and you're probably lost somewhere in your bits and bytes." She pointed to the table. "Don't think I didn't notice the tablet, the laptop, and the folder with your notes for the video game you're working on. Your boss isn't making you finish it while you're in the hospital, is he?"

"My boss wouldn't ask anything that he wouldn't do himself."

"That's not an answer, Reeves. Yes or no. Are you trying to work and heal at the same time?"

"Can't I do both?"

"No." She shook her head and drew out the word. "One or the other and right now, it is the other." She looked up at the clock. "Visiting hours are almost over. Has he been here or is he coming?"

"Kinda both."

"Then I'll kinda wait until someone comes to throw me out, just in case."

"You don't intend to kill him or anything, do you?"

"That all depends on Rashesh and how he comes through that door—empty handed or loaded for video bear."

Footsteps made her glance toward the door. One of

the nurses, an older woman named Rae, stood there. "Fifteen minutes, and this time, I mean it." She walked toward Kinley. "This man needs his rest. His rehab is kicking up a final notch in the morning." She set a fresh pitcher of water on the bed table. "The doctors are almost done working on your face," she said, "so now the rehab team will give you a program to work on the rest." She turned back to Kinley. "And I'll be watching you. No sneaking back in like you do every other day."

Kinley chuckled. "I'm sorry. I'm leaving as soon as I'm sure no one else is coming in."

"I'm holding you to that," Rae said as she walked out.

Kinley stood and straightened the blankets on the bed. "You know what?"

"What?"

"You sound stronger every day, but Nurse Ratchet is right. You need to keep moving those legs to get back your strength completely. The sooner you mend, the sooner you can return to your normal life."

He did not want his life to return to normal. He wanted Kinley. "That's exactly what I told the doctor this morning. I do want out."

"I can't blame you for being impatient. I mean if I was cooped up in here for as long as you've been, I'd be crazy by now."

"There were a lot of pieces to put back together, Kin. It takes time."

"I know."

Her voice sounded like a faraway whisper. "Don't worry, Kin. I'm not Humpty Dumpty. Everything will be in place and working when the doctors are done. At least that's what they tell me."

"Okay, just for the record, you still owe me Chinese." She bent down toward him.

He saw her wispy bangs, the faint spray of freckles across her nose, her soft mouth. He knew she was looking for a spot to kiss him just as she did every other night.

Before the accident, they hadn't kissed much. And when they did, the kiss was friendly and quick. But since his hospitalization, she made a point to search for a spot somewhere among the bandages on every visit.

Her blue-eyed gaze rested on his as she leaned closer. For almost two years, he imagined her kissing him every night, but not because of this. He proved himself to be a trusted friend, someone who was different from all the other guys she dated, someone who cared for her as a person first and appreciated her as a woman without thinking of sexual intimacy all the time. But the accident did more than give her a reason to decide she could express an honest and affectionate gesture. It had complicated matters to no end.

Her lips touched his, softer than satin and gentler than the sigh he heard in her voice. He pushed his conflicting thoughts to the back of his mind. He caught the scent of the perfume she liked to wear, saw her silky blond hair sweep down in pale curls, and heard the rustle of her suit. The first time she kissed him, all he had to do was brace himself because the kiss was over in two seconds. But every time since, she stretched the time they kissed. Past two seconds, past five, past the point of a goodnight kiss between friends. Or so, he hoped. He was very careful not to touch her, not to move, almost not to breathe.

When she finally moved away, she locked her gaze

on his for almost as long as the kiss lasted, and then quickly moved away.He could see a soft pink color flush her cheeks. *Now! Say something. Now.*

Rashesh emerged from the hallway, two more laptops under his arm, and carrying a box full of papers.

"Jack, the investors…" When he saw Kinley, he stopped talking and his eyes rounded. "I didn't expect you here."

Kinley's gaze moved from the computers to the box and then to Rashesh's eyes. "Apparently not."

Jack hit the button and raised the head of his bed. "Kinley, I…"

She turned. "I got this. Lay back down." She watched to make sure he did before turning to Rashesh. "I cannot believe you came here, work in hand, no doubt expecting Jack to finish something you screwed up." She tossed her hand toward him. "That man can star in a Return of the Mummy movie, the cast is barely off his arm, and he has an obstacle course to run in the morning. Get someone else to work out the kinks with your toys." Squaring her shoulders, she pointed to the door. "Out."

Rashesh took a step back and banged into the door frame, the laptops nearly falling. He struggled to save them as he spoke. "But Jack wanted me to bring him this stuff."

Kinley turned slowly to Jack, arms crossed over her chest. "No doubt. But not tonight." She grabbed Rashesh by the arm.

He struggled to regain the balance of everything he brought.

She ushered him out the door. "We're leaving together. Tell Nurse Ratchet goodnight. I love you.

Sleep tight."

Jack could hear her lecturing Rashesh as her heels clicked down the hospital hallway. He sank down into the pillow and squeezed closed his eyes. What on earth could he do? Along with her new habit of kissing him every night was the light sounding *I love you* when she left.

A few minutes in which nothing occupied his brain but Kinley's face passed.

Then Rae walked in with his meds. "Hi, honey. I see I scared away your sister."

"Confession, Rae. She isn't my sister."

Rae laughed. "She didn't fool me one bit. She came every day you were still in la-la land. All fussing over you, tucking in the sheets, worrying about all sorts of things. Sisters are concerned about their brothers, but not like that." She wrapped Jack's arm in a blood pressure cuff and pumped it up. "Of all your visitors, she's my favorite. Such a sweetheart, that one. She makes us all laugh. Mr. Riley in 503 thinks she's as cute as a button. He wants to take her home. Eighty-three or not, he can still appreciate the ladies."

Jack laughed. "I'll make sure to tell him that he can't have her."

Rae held up the thermometer cannula until Jack opened his mouth. "She won't last long out in the single world, honey. To paraphrase Beyoncé, if you like it, put a ring on it."

"Our relationship is a bit more complicated than that," Jack mumbled, the thermometer bouncing up and down against his lips.

Rae checked the temperature, recorded it, and turned back. "I hope you figure it out in time."

Jack blew out a long breath of air. "I hope you're right."

"Dr. Wheeler is letting you try solid food tomorrow. Keep it down, and I think you can go home in a few days." She arched the stethoscope around her neck and rummaged around on the meds cart she brought in. "I have some juice and a couple of pills for you, and then I'm on to your rival's room." She winked. "I'd hold on to that lady if I were you. She's special."

"That she is," Jack agreed as Rae left.

He sipped his juice and ignored the pills. Pulling himself up and then twisting to a sitting position, he found the pair of ratty old slippers Kinley brought and slowly stood. He shuffled the five steps to the window. The dizzy sensation that accompanied every step told him he had a long way to go until he was anywhere near ready to go home.

Bracing both hands on the windowsill, he scanned the hospital parking lot below. He had hoped Kinley circled and she would be coming back to see him. But only Rashesh's distinctive VW pulled into an empty slot. He straightened to walk back to the bed and caught his reflection in the glass.

The tall, leaner man he saw stunned him. Okay, he had always been tall, but he gave up the battle for lean a few years ago. The body he saw could be a stranger's from the outline in the glass. The new thinner and straighter posture probably resulted from physical therapy that became a part of his daily routine since he'd been allowed out of bed. That and the liquid diet he'd been forced to endure. Just looking at the reflection made him a lot more edgy about what lurked under the bandages. The plastic surgeon repeatedly assured him the reconstruction had gone fabulously, and he would look great. But who would he look like?

At first, he hadn't cared, as long as his scars wouldn't scare children and make women stare in both horror and pity. But now, he did care.

Something strong was building with Kinley, something deeper than friendship. She wasn't behaving the same way around him since the accident. Their friendship now felt as though they had both gotten knocked around somehow. The time they spent together was richer and a lot more meaningful.

He loved her being part of his healing, loved the way she made sure he had everything he needed, loved the way she had opened up and trusted him with her thoughts and feelings. Lately, he started to believe she might love him as a man, not a buddy. Once he got home, he needed to be sure their relationship would not be damaged by what he had to tell her or how he looked.

But right now, he had little time for second guesses about how he had handled things for the past two years and returned to the bed. Rashesh, loaded down with two laptops and a messenger bag filled with papers, stepped through the doorway. He set one computer on the bed table and the other on Jack's lap once he slid over the worn metal chair. "Okay," Rashesh said, powering up the laptop. "*Gaming Magazine* is testing War Zone III as we speak. The game will be featured in a fall issue when we get final word on the release date."

The screen on the laptop in front of Jack burst on. "All the kinks are out of level twelve?"

Rashesh nodded. "Kinley's brother found the

glitch." He kept talking. Jack didn't respond, so he closed his laptop. "What's up?"

Jack gave his head a small shake. "Nothing." He pecked at the keyboard, then looked up. "What did you tell Kinley's brother?"

"I asked Mike if he could help out until you were up and running again."

"And that's all?"

"Yes." Silence hung thick in the air until Rashesh reached over and closed the lid on Jack's laptop.

Jack had to look up.

"She still doesn't know about you and the company, does she?"

Slowly, Jack shook his head. "I was going to tell her." He pointed to his face. "The night this happened. Now, how can I?"

"*War Zone III* is predicted to be the biggest game ever. Pre-orders are through the roof, and the buzz on the internet is incredible."

Jack saw caution roll into Rashesh's eyes. "I know that look. What else?"

"The blog's been buzzing with speculation about you and the accident. Apparently, a couple of gaming fans work here and connected the proverbial dots. In a few days, someone, somewhere, will post on FindOut.com or, worse case, social media will explode with the news of your accident and new face. You have to come clean with Kinley before she reads it on the web."

"She doesn't do the social networks."

"But what if her brother sees a computer-generated comparison of your before and after face on somebody's gaming blog, speculating the CEO of

Gaming International is now a hottie? Blood is thicker as they say. He will ask questions or say something."

Jack felt his stomach drop to somewhere in the hospital basement. "What am I supposed to say?"

Rashesh grimaced. "The truth is always the best. Try 'Kinley, you know that Rashesh Patel guy? The one you think is such a slave driver? Truth is, I don't work for him, but he works for me. Gaming International and the Nerd Herd. They're mine. I own the companies. They are about to go public on the stock exchange, making me and Rashesh even richer than we already are. I swear I wanted to tell you but I ran into something, or rather something ran into me, and the timing was never quite right after that.'"

Anxiety bubbled in Jack's stomach as he listened. He glanced at the window before turning back to Rashesh. "And then, when I'm done confessing a two-year lie, that's when she either hits me or walks out of my life forever."

Rashesh nodded slowly. "I would probably do both."

Chapter Three

After fine-tuning a few last minor glitches in the video game, Rashesh left.

Jack sank against his hospital pillow and squeezed his eyes closed. An anxious, edgy feeling settled into his stomach. Now he had two major things in his life to fix.

His medical mess would improve on its own if he followed doctors' orders. Even now, all the broken parts were healing just fine. From his new bionic knee to his broken jaw and reconstructive surgery, except for a few bouts of sudden pain, he actually felt pretty good, all things considered. The liquid diet and physical therapy had shrunk down his body, but he stilled tired easily, and really couldn't build up all that much strength when his diet had the consistency of tapioca.

But getting out of the hole he had dug for himself with Kinley before the accident would not be so easy. He would work on the trust issues that would surely arise almost as hard as he would undoubtedly work in rehab to make sure Kinley stayed in his life. If she even wanted anything to do with him after he confessed the past two years had been constructed like a world in one of his popular video games.

He turned off his bedside light and stared at the dark ceiling. Before Kinley, he had all but given up on having any type of serious relationship. Sure, he had a lot of female friends. His average looks, his good-natured, and even-keel personality didn't pressure them into anything, but they didn't inspire anything either. Before Kinley, he had been pretty sure he was incapable of inspiring any female in any way.

So far, he'd only had one or two relationships that he considered one step up from friend. None of the maybe three others he could think of ever got any more involved. True, while none ended in marriage, none ended badly. They all just fizzled like a bottle of champagne left uncorked. The girls that "befriended" him did so because he was safe and never asked for anything. When he tried to get closer, helped them in little ways, or brought flowers or gifts, he'd get a thank you and a little kiss on his cheek. Then they'd go out with one of the hot, happening guys he could never be.

Someday, he wanted to get married and have children. But worse than being alone was being with someone just to have a body in the same house so he wouldn't grow old alone. He couldn't justify that in any way, shape, or form. As far as he was concerned, being with someone just because you thought the time was right would be the most painful type of loneliness.

Before the accident, he thought, no, *hoped*, Kinley could feel something more than friendship. If he had to guess, maybe, she could be two steps above friend if he did everything just right. He also guessed she had no idea he was already in love with her. But now a future with her felt all wrong and hopeless. He had lived a two-year lie because he was too self-interested to tell her the truth.

Together, they looked like someone had paired a Ford with a Jaguar. He could look at a Jag, even maybe dream about it, but he could never actually touch it. Same thing with Kinley.

He sighed heavily and closed his eyes. Since he got the high school bullies to stop picking on him by acting like a bumbling, good-natured dolt no matter what anyone said, he'd managed by becoming invisible. He morphed into the kind of guy who faded into the woodwork so no one noticed. He survived by shrinking from the attention and moving forward.

With a shaking hand, he touched the bandage on his face. What would he find underneath? All he wanted right now was to go home, go back to work, and have nothing change. But that would never be possible. The bandages on his face reminded him of that every day.

****

Kinley walked up to the door of Jack's house with a whole lot of feelings rolling around inside. She could hardly believe a few months had passed since she got the awful news about Jack's accident. But time raced forward, and today was unveiling day.

After getting no answer to the knock, she poked her head inside. "Hey, it's me! I hope you aren't playing video games, or worse, working. Today is an important day!"

"I'm here and I am working," Jack called back.

She shook her head and closed the door. Technically, he was still on medical leave, but she couldn't convince him to take it slow. She knew Rashesh kept bringing him work, and the pile on his desk grew and receded almost every day. Reminding him the doctor told him to take it easy fell on deaf ears.

She glanced around the kitchen to figure out how

he was doing on this very important day. The counter was littered with breakfast toast crumbs, something he loved in the morning, more so now that he was back on solid food. Some midnight snack dishes were in the sink, and a tidy pile of mail and magazines sat on the table. Personally, she didn't trust anyone who did not immediately open his or her mail, but Jack was something special so she would forgive that annoying habit.

She headed straight for his office and heard the clicking of computer keys before she reached it. He'd been working non-stop on the next version of some action video game almost since the day he came home from the hospital. She knew he was a hard-core perfectionist, and probably only pretended to wrap up things for the night and go to bed, but actually went back to work as soon as she left.

She stopped at the office doorway. The closed wooden blinds shut out the midday sun and made the room bleak. She could see Jack hunched over a glowing laptop computer. He had on his New York Giants football shirt, his favorite, so desperately frayed that he should have replaced it three seasons ago. He was obviously concentrating so hard he hadn't heard her come in.

For a while, she watched him in silence, a lump forming in her throat. In the beginning, he had been her friend who saved her from the deleted-file-black-hole, but slowly, over time, her feelings had drastically changed. Maybe the realization hit hard of how close she had been to losing him forever. Or maybe the way he coped with what had been handed him without so much as an unkind word had warmed her soul. Maybe all the time they spent together every day since he left the hospital had become all that more precious, or the way he made her laugh despite all the pain that pounded him. Whatever happened, she knew she could never go back to just being friends. The way she felt about him had changed forever.

At first, she'd seen him as a friend, a brainy, slightly out-of-shape guy, mainly because he kept on reminding her that was who he was. She considered him her CPU knight in shining armor, fixer of data disasters, loyal friend, and the best listener in the universe. She'd seen Jack in lots of everyday roles—all of them wonderfully thoughtful.

But until she almost lost him, she never really dwelled on Jack as a man. A single man. A male human being in her life to complement her female side.

Though she had reservations and serious misgivings about screwing up such a special friendship, she couldn't help thinking beyond it. She could not deny that each day she spent alone with Jack, more emotions emerged that had never been there before—thoughts of family and forever. She barely knew what to do, she only knew she had to do something.

But for now, she'd take it slow, one day at a time. And today, she had a very important unveiling. She knocked on the wall to get his attention. "Hey, you have a doctor's appointment today, remember?"

Jack didn't move or take his fingers from the keyboard. "I didn't forget. The appointment is at two."

She walked up behind him, her hands molding around his shoulders and neck. As she expected, his muscles were knotted. No question, he had been sitting at the computer a long time. She started a slow massage, careful not the touch the bandages. "Do you even know what time it is now?"

He shrugged. "Nine? Ten?"

"It's noon."

"Ah." He rolled his neck. "That feels great."

In response, she pressed harder, pushing to release the knots in his shoulders. Then suddenly, as though her female hormones had been released from prison, she became conscious of the warmth of his skin and of her response. Her mind slowly conjured up a whole lot of pictures, all of them wild and inappropriate.

"It can't be noon," Jack said, "I just started working."

"Probably at day break." The knots in his back had eased. Reluctantly, she dropped her hands. "Time to get dressed." She spun his chair around. Her gaze raced around his bandaged face, and she adjusted the glasses on his bandaged nose as an excuse as to why she was staring. "At least you will keep these in place once the gauze comes off. I cannot wait to see what's under all that white. I'm going with you."

"No, you're not," he said, shaking his head.

Was that panic she heard in his voice? "I want to go."

"Rashesh is driving me. No need to waste your time in a doctor's waiting room. This post-op could take a few hours." He turned his chair back and hit the save button on the computer.

She shrugged. "It's the least that slave-driver could do." If he didn't want her to go, she'd stay here. Even for a man as unconcerned with his appearance as Jack, she could tell he wanted to see the finished product first, alone. The reveal would be traumatic enough.

She'd give him that. "Okay, I'll wait here." She waited until he turned back and then touched his bandaged cheek. "It will be fine," she reassured.

"Promise?"

The doubt in his voiced roared. "More than promise."

"The plastic surgeons told me that everything went fine, and the reconstruction was successful, but you never know. They showed me some computerized pictures that approximated what they had done. But, when the bandages are off, I could have a roadmap of scars across my cheeks. You might be ashamed to be seen with me."

She saw emotions riot in his eyes. This was the first time she had ever heard real fear in his voice when he talked about his new face. "I could never be ashamed to be seen with you, Jack."

He smiled as much as the bandages allowed.

But she noticed the smile didn't reach his eyes. She heard a car pull up outside—probably Rashesh. "But maybe if you continue to wear that shirt, it could be another story. Get changed, get going, and get back. I can't wait to see the results of your tune up."

****

Kinley paced the hallway. Jack's homecoming was taking too long. She began to call Rashesh on his cell when she heard a car pull into the driveway. She walked to the front door and took a deep breath, locking a smile on her face, intent on saying all the right things—no matter what the outcome of Jack's surgery—and opened the door.

She felt her smile turn into a round, open-mouthed circle that let out a soft gasp. "What have they done to you?" The words slipped out before she could stop them. She had steeled herself for scars and for the fact Jack might look a little different. She fully intended to help him cope with any changes and not let him feel any different. But Jack's new face was a total shock, and nothing could have prepared her for what she saw.

Chapter Four

Jack expected Kinley to be surprised with his "new" face. Anyone who knew him would be surprised. But with her eyes wide and her gaze focused on his face, she looked shocked. A huge lump formed in his throat.

He tried to keep his voice calm. "I won't look like this forever, Kin. The doctor told me the swelling will go down and the bruising will go away in a few weeks."

Kinley took a step backward. "It's not the swelling or the bruises." Her gaze stayed focused on his face.

Rashesh looked from Kinley to Jack. "This is my cue to leave. Call me if you need anything," his fading voice said as he headed for his car.

Kinley waved a half-hearted goodbye, but she didn't look away from Jack's face as she did. A siren screamed in the distance. She didn't look away. Children ran up and down the sidewalk, and mothers' voices called to them. She didn't look away. The newspaper boy hurled a paper that landed in the shrubs. She still didn't look away.

"You're staring." He expected a reaction to his new look, but Kinley's gaze locked on his face like a missile heading to a laser-guided target made him sweat. "Do I look that bad?"

"No. I just would never have known it was you," she continued, her unwavering gaze never left his face.

"If I hadn't heard your voice, I would have thought you were a stranger."

"It's still me, honest."

"Have you seen yourself?"

"Briefly. Do you think you can get used to this face?"

She stepped closer, her hand extended, but stopped short of touching him. "I can't get over this. You're....perfect." Her hand retracted, and she rested it on her chest near her heart. Then she began to backpedal. "Not that you weren't a looker before, of course."

His brows furrowed as he decided Kinley must have thought she hurt his feelings. "Stop, Kinley. Don't worry about saying something wrong. I feel kind of wrong myself." *That's an understatement.* He felt like someone hit him in the gut when he saw his new face in the mirror at the doctor's office. But whether his face was handsome or ugly didn't matter. The only thing that mattered was the image wasn't him. The face he grew up with, the face everyone knew had vanished along with the face he had hoped Kinley would forgive once he told her what he still needed to tell. Gone was the face he dreamed she could fall in love with someday replaced by a stranger's face.

He had been so deep in thought he hadn't noticed she touched his cheek. "It must be a bit unnerving to look so different."

He walked to the hall mirror. "Beyond that...it's eerie."

She walked up behind him. "But you do look great. The only scar I can see is the one in your left eyebrow."

"There are plenty of scars, but the doctor did a

great job of keeping them near my hairline or under my jaw." With one hand, he swept the hair back from his face. "The doctor suggested I keep my hair longer so that most of the scars won't show." He hadn't had a haircut since before the accident. All the thick, unruly hair hanging around his face and collar just added to the ridiculousness he felt. He had always worn his hair super short. Maybe the style looked a bit geeky, but he liked that it didn't take much care or maintenance beyond sitting in a barber chair every few weeks. He let the hair fall back across his forehead. Now he might actually have to go to a stylist. He didn't even know one.

He turned to face her. "I stopped to get gas on the way home. I've been buying gas at that station for years. The guy didn't even know me." He could hear the restless, impatient tone in his voice, but he couldn't help it. "I walked into the doctor's office being me, and I walked out someone else. I feel like I'm in a movie on the SyFy Channel, and I don't know how it will end."

Kinley bit down on her lip and looked at him. "I had hoped the changes wouldn't be hard for you, but it sounds like just the opposite. Women change their hairstyles and go for makeovers, so to a point, it would be different for us. We love change. It gives us an emotional lift. If we don't like the style, we grow our hair back, or change the makeup. But for you. You didn't have a say in your new look." She reached out. "I see something here." She raised her hand and pushed his hair behind one ear.

Jack knew what she saw. On the underside of his jaw were the angriest-looking scars. Couple those with the bruising that made him look like a raccoon and the jagged scar that cut through his eyebrow, and he looked like a modern day Frankenstein. Though Kinley's fingertips barely touched his chin, his skin felt hypersensitive, probably from the new skin finally exposed to light and air. He controlled a natural impulse to stop the burning sensation by moving away from her touch, afraid if he did, she might not do it again.

He glanced again into the mirror. His face was really nothing horrible to look at—just different. He had a square chin now and a rather aquiline nose. He didn't think his cheekbones had changed, but they looked completely different in a face that used to be round and pudgy but had now been sculpted with thought and planning. The plastic surgeon had been totally ecstatic with the unveiling. He, however, could not be sure he shared the doctor's approval.

But what Jack did approve of was Kinley being this close, touching him as though he was a most important piece of art. His pulse rose and bucked as she moved her fingertips gently across his jaw line. He tried to justify his feelings by telling himself any guy would react this way to a woman being this sensitive to the situation. But he knew it would be a total lie. Okay, she was insightful and sure, her compassion was a wonderful quality, but who would he be kidding? His hormones moved at warp speed because he had fallen madly and desperately in love with Kinley.

His whole world always went into total metamorphosis when she was around. She was the only one who could make him put down the video game he was testing, make him end the conference calls with the buyers, and even make him forget to get into work early to work out a kink in a troublesome game level. His hormones, once content to sleep through any day with normal male-female events, always woke up and wanted to party when Kinley was nearby.

She stepped back and rocked on her heels, still studying his face. "I don't think you'll have many scars once you're healed, but right now, some places look plenty painful."

"I'll be fine," he assured.

"The area stitched together near your ear looks like it's pretty sore."

"It's nothing."

"Maybe nothing compared to being tossed around the front of your car, but it's still more than nothing. Good thing you won't be going back to work for a few weeks."

"Ah, Kin?"

She crossed her arms in front of her. "Don't tell me that slave driver, Rashesh, wants you back sooner. Because you certainly are not ready."

A clear warning laced her tone. The question he wanted to ask her had nothing to do with work. But with her standing so close, anything he wanted to say flew completely out of his mind. She said he looked perfect, but he knew he didn't. Kinley, on the other hand, always looked that way. Though the jeans and shirt she wore were nothing fancy, they looked great on her. The crisp air had painted her cheeks a soft rose, and the wind played with her hair, making her honey blond curls dance around her face. Her blue eyes looked softer than silk. She looked…kissable.

Then suddenly, he remembered all the kisses she gave him in the hospital. There, he had bandages and tubes surrounding him, encasing him, and he could never touch her or kiss her back. Now, bandage free, he could kiss her the way he always wanted to, but he wouldn't. Not until he told her what he had to tell her. Until then, kissing Kinley was on the strictly forbidden list—the kind of list you write in ink so you don't forget it.

He would hold on to the memory of how her mouth tasted on his and dream about kissing her without bandages on. Without his permission, he focused on that daydream, and his mouth curved in a smile.

Kinley snapped her fingers in front of his eyes. "Hey. Come back."

"I'm here." He realized he had been staring at her like a thief in a jewelry store. Mentally, he whacked himself upside his head to get the vision out of his mind. "What did you want?"

Kinley narrowed her gaze. "It was you who wanted something. You started to ask me a question then stopped. Then you got a really strange look on your new face, like you were somewhere on the third moon of Jupiter."

He may as well be there for all the work he'd have to do to get their relationship back to normal. He struggled to return to earth. "I just feel sort of awkward. New body because of the PT, and new face because of the windshield in my old car. I don't know what I should do first, but I know I need you to help me with something."

"Sure. Anything. What can I do?"

He hesitated. *Don't ask me that. I just may tell you.*

Kinley dipped her head and waited. After a few seconds, she said, "You want me to help you get a new car? You know how I am with mechanical stuff."

He shook his head. "Not a car, something a little more personal."

Kinley put her hands on her hips. "Jack, we've known each other for two years now." She laughed. "Unless you're hiding a secret life, talking about something personal shouldn't make you act like you're asking me out on a first date."

His stomach dropped to the ground—lower if he could have found a nearby hole. *Nope, not a good time for confessions.* Seems like he would have to delay his plan to come clean and switch to something else. He looked away so she couldn't read the turmoil in his eyes. "You've done so much for me since the accident. I almost hate to ask you for another favor." He looked up and felt his glasses slipping down his nose. He pushed them up with his index finger. He saw Kinley's smile brighten.

"You want to get contact lenses, and you want me to go with you."

Good enough. Go with it. "That's it. My old glasses don't fit my new nose. They keep sliding down. Very annoying. Will you? I'd do the laser thing, but I've had enough cutting on body parts to last me a while."

"Of course I'll go. What are friends for?

He grabbed the hem of the shirt he wore. "And maybe help get me some new clothes. These sweat pants almost went south when I got out of the car."

Kinley covered her mouth with the fingertips of her right hand. "Oh my. I suddenly realize what you're facing. This is worse than anything you have ever faced before. Worse than the monsters in your closet when you were a kid or any kind of torture you could imagine. You have to go shopping."

He winced. "Never say that word out loud. I have a better idea."

"And that would be?" she asked smiling.

At that moment, Jack decided nothing better existed on earth than one of her purely female grins. "How about I keep my battered body and new face at home, and you go out and shop *for* me?" He barreled on, sweetening the pot before she answered. "Of course, you would be aptly rewarded. I could pay your home shopping bill." He tsked. "I've seen it. Not quite the national debt, but close. This is also how I know you're a pretty adept shopper."

"How do you know? Did you hack into my QVC account with your super powers?"

"No, you dropped your bill on the kitchen floor a few weeks before…" He punched a fist into the air. "You know, ka-pow." She laughed, and he thought he heard angels singing. A corny romantic notion, but he didn't care. "Hey, this is a serious business deal I'm offering. If not that, how about I buy you some kind of girlie doodads?"

"Doodads?" She chuckled harder.

"Or a few weeks in Hawaii? I'm serious. You can have anything you want, just don't make me go to the mall."

"Stop." She picked up an accent pillow from the sofa and tossed it at him. "Of course I'll help you. Free of charge, too. You don't have to bribe me. But seriously, you won't get cooties or anything by walking into a department store."

"I know but I read somewhere nature gave each gender a specific evolutionary goal. A man shopping goes against that master plan. We are the hunters, the protectors. You and your kind are the nesters. You must shop to make your nest. If the roles get screwed up, our species just may die out. Would you want to take on that responsibility?" He crossed his arms in front of him. "I don't think so."

Kinley waved her hands in front of her. "Far be it from me to end mankind as we know it. I'll shop for you but I have to warn you, you still may have to visit a tailor. You've lost so much weight that neither of us know what size you are."

"Let's just guess. Bring stuff here, and I'll try it on. What fits stays and what doesn't, goes back."

"That might work for some things, but not for the suits."

Jack's eyebrows arched in surprise. "You're buying me suits?"

"Of course. I guess you haven't had time to keep up with your own work, but my brother tells me that War Zone III is through the roof. You'll be out of tech support and into game development in no time."

Jack's mouth dropped open. "How often do you talk to your brother?" He felt a bead of sweat run down his spine.

"He's my brother. I talk to him every day. Why?"

"What do you talk about every day?"

"Mostly War Zone III. Seems that it's the hottest game on the planet right now. Mikey has been following the sales, and stores can't keep the thing in stock." She rubbed her thumb across the back of her fingers. "You're making Rashesh a rich man. Why wouldn't he promote you?"

Because I'm his boss. He could have taken this

opportunity to tell her, but didn't. Too much was going on to have to think about an explanation or dodge whatever she might find to throw. Admitting his two-year lie would not end well right now. Clearing his conscience moved down on his priority list.

He gave his head a little shake and straightened his spine. "Worrying about a promotion will have to wait. For now, how about I just give you my credit cards, and you start shopping?

"Let me get some magazines. We can go through the ads, and you can at least give me an idea of what you might want."

"I got that covered. A new Giants football jersey, a Devils hockey jersey and…"

"A Mets shirt," she finished then threw her hands in the air. "This will be a challenge."

He watched her walk to her car, get in, and shoot him a good-bye with the wave of her hand. When he waved back, he accidentally hit the side of his face. He winced. Some areas were still really tender.

He smiled. Tender. Another word that reminded him of Kinley. He shook his head. He was so the nerd. Just the thought of her could bring him to his knees. Heck, her smile could bring any man to his knees, and he wanted to be that man.

For a long time now, his day had been occupied with all things relating to the accident. The physical therapy, the weak and exhausted feeling, and the whole business of getting a new face was a twenty-four-seven kind of blur. But now, all that was over, the only thing that remained was the fear Kinley might not be comfortable with the new Jack Reeves. The *entire* new Jack Reeves, CEO of Gaming International that had just exploded at the public offering. Rashesh hinted he might even make the *Forbes* list of the richest men. He had to tell Kinley soon. Before the magazine came out, at least.

He had to concentrate. He hadn't meant to ask her to shop, but he didn't want to reestablish himself as a nerd in her eyes. With all that had happened and all that would happen from now on, he knew he could no longer be the guy who never noticed how he looked, the bookworm guy, the brainy guy who could write computer code and fix anything that broke. He had to move forward and get used to his new life—Brad Pitt face and all. The shopping thing was a start, but he still had a long way to go.

****

Kinley pulled into a parking spot at the mall, unable to remember how she even got there. What she did remember vividly was Jack's new face. Though still a little bruised in some spots and a nice color of pinky-red in others, his face was…there could be no other word…his face was perfect. Textbook perfect. Like the doctors heard her talking about Brad Pitt, Johnny Depp, and Alex O'Loughlin, cut out all the good parts of their faces, taped them together, and used the result as a schematic for what they wanted to accomplish. And if that had been the plan, they had done it well.

Although she felt ecstatic his long bandaged journey was finally over, she had to face the tiny part of her that felt suddenly afraid. Would Perfect Jack still be the person who set out to get her some *kung pao* chicken but got an extreme makeover—total body edition—instead? How would he respond when his friends, co-workers and yes, with apologies to Beyoncé, all the single ladies, reacted to his new look?

Because once the daters and the cougars got a look at the new, improved Jack Reeves, he would never again be the last one in line.

Chapter Five

A little later, Kinley burst into Jack's living room, six shopping bags in hand. Of course, he wasn't there waiting. She could hear the sound of video game war coming from his office. She set the bags on the couch and set off to liberate him from whatever evil lurked in the world he built this time.

"Hey," she said, leaning on the door sill. "When you finish saving the world for democracy or whatever you're doing, your new clothes await. But I have to warn you, your next credit card statement might just rival the national debt."

He had his back toward her and she could see his shoulders tense as he nudged the controller to the right and hit three of the enemy with a fire bomb. "I don't care how much the clothes cost. Besides, I'm sure most of them will be going back anyway."

"Don't think so. I have impeccable taste, you know." Finally, the sounds of battle stopped.

"That I do know."

She motioned with her forefinger. "Then follow me." She walked back to the living room and began laying out the clothes, suddenly nervous. She only bought what she thought he might need, but now feared Jack might turn and run when he saw all the packages. And she hadn't even factored in the styles and colors she'd chosen with not a team logo T-shirt or a pair of sweat pants in sight.

"Okay, let's see it." He stood behind her and looked over her shoulder.

"Brace yourself." She turned. But this close, when she saw him, all other thoughts, all the guilt, and all the stuff she planned on saying went right out of her head. Jack's new face meant she had some adjusting of her own to do. He didn't just look perfect; he was now an absolute gorgeous hunk.

Quickly, she forced neutrality into her expression. He did not need to know how much his appearance affected her. Enough people would were going to be shocked and make all sorts of comments. Enough people might suddenly see someone who has been right in front of them all along. She needed to help him in the adjustment process, not come off like someone who cared about the outside as opposed to the inside. There would be enough of those people coming into his life shortly.

She stepped back so he could see the packages. "Well, here it all is!"

"Geeze Louise." Jack pointed at the mounds of shopping bags, counting them. "Is there anything left at the mall?"

"I only bought what I thought you needed." She looked at the clothing mounds on the sofa. "Looks as though you needed quite a bit." With a grin, she moved to a side chair and sat. "Well go ahead, forage."

He stood in the middle of the room, scratching his head. "I didn't mean for you to go through all this trouble. A shirt or two would have been enough." He shrugged, his hand slowly dropping. "Now what?"

She smiled at the simplicity of his question. He

was truly the most unpretentious man she had ever met. She pointed. "Now, you go through everything and tell me what you like, and what you don't."

"By the look of things, that could take hours. I'm sure everything is great, so let's just leave everything where it is for now."

She grabbed his hand and pulled him toward the nearest bag. "Oh no, you don't. These new clothes will not bite you." She picked up the Macy's bag and hooked it over his hand. "Open."

"I intend to look at everything later, honest."

That's a lie. Jack probably wanted nothing more than to get back to blowing up bad guys in the video game. She continued talking until he gave in and began rummaging through the bags.

As she expected, he looked up from each one mumbling something that sounded like either 'This is perfect' or 'You have such great taste' and 'I really like this' before moving onto the next bag. He hadn't noticed anything about the clothes as he held them in front of him in a sad attempt to keep things moving, but she did. She could picture how the style and color would look, and very much liked what she imagined. His clothes had been just to the right of pitiful before—outdated, ill fitting, and downright ugly. While she was sure Jack wouldn't want to look like a *GQ* model, he had every reason to look a little trendier and not so much thrift store.

He'd never been a bad-looking guy. He just never stood out from all the other average-looking guys in the world. The extra weight he carried around his middle and the self-cut hair style made him appear much older. His pre-accident round-shouldered posture draped in the dated clothes he liked to wear added to his geeky image. Then Jack was the kind of guy who you could look right at in a crowd and never see. But not now. Kinley wondered how he would react when he caught an unfamiliar woman's eye for the first time. With his new looks, he definitely would.

He finished emptying the last bag and brought it to her. "Kin, I owe you big time. But some of these things are just not me."

Jack's expression looked that of a true martyr. She tried to hide a smile but failed. "Which ones?"

"I sorted the clothes into two piles. The stuff on the left should go back, and the stuff on the right can stay."

She looked over his shoulder. Only a few shirts and one pair of Dockers lay on the floor to the right. She spun him around and gently nudged him forward. "You gave it your best shot, but let's try this again—only this time, together."

An hour later, the piles had shifted and only a few things needed returning. Kinley folded the last shirt, and an idea formed in her head. "I'm supposed to be meeting Judy for dinner tonight. Why don't you try out your new clothes and join us?"

He shook his head. "I don't think so. I have a problem with level nine on War Zone IV."

"And I have a problem with the beginning level of Jack Reeves Two. Seems the main character isn't making progress."

"Probably just a glitch. Better shut down for a while."

Kinley grinned. *He's not getting off that easy.* "You always told me the way to figure out a kink is to make a note and keep moving forward. That's pretty sound advice. Come with us. You'll be fine."

She could tell by the way Jack shifted from foot to foot that he was not comfortable going out of the house just yet. Though a lot of people visited him in the hospital, no one had seen him since the bandages were removed. Going out with her and her BFF would give him a chance to ease into his new face. She and Judy would help him with that. Being with friends to shore up his confidence was something he needed right now.

"I don't think so."

She knew him. Stubborn and strong-willed, he would not change his mind unless she got him to believe going out would be a great unselfish act. The man had a hapless chivalrous streak. "Come on, Jack, you'd be doing me a favor. Judy might be bringing her latest guy, and I'd feel like a third wheel. Having you along would even things out. It's Judy's turn to drive and if she and her squeeze wanted to do a duo thing, I would be stranded with no way to get home."

He made the familiar telephone gesture. "Call me. I'll pick you up."

She might be losing the battle. "Truth then. I feel a bit awkward going. They are a new couple, and I'll look like the conspicuous dateless friend. Couldn't you come just this one time? I did do all that shopping, so you do owe me." She could tell by his face he was weakening.

"Well, I can understand the dateless friend thing. I've played that role more times than I care to admit."

"So, you'll come?" She knew he would give in eventually, but crossed her fingers behind her back to call upon whatever luck may be floating in the air to help him cave. He'd never turned down anything she'd asked yet.

He nodded. "I feel as though I'll regret this."

"Not in your life. It'll be fun. You'll see."

****

Kinley dug into the salsa with the last whole taco chip left in the bowl, happy that Jack appeared to actually be enjoying himself.

"Anyone for another round? I'm buying," he said.

A few female voices from the next table combined into a chorus. "We'll buy if you come over here and join us, sweet thing."

A flush of red ran up Jack's neck. Kinley chuckled at his reaction. *Sweet thing*. Jack Reeves. Before today, who would have thought that? She saw him shoot them a rather awkward smile before looking back at her with desperation in his eyes. *Time to rescue the man.*

Reaching over, she looped her arm around his neck. "Honey, just get us something and let the nice ladies find some other way to get refills." She turned to the all-female table and mouthed, *He's taken.*

Jack pushed back from the table and took orders before winding his way to the bar.

He did look good. Kinley watched as a woman "accidentally" bumped into him and attempted to start a conversation. He looked better than good. He'd changed into some of the clothes she bought him. Nothing fancy, just nice-fitting jeans and a black shirt. The shirt made his shoulders look a mile wide, and the jeans cupped his newly in-shape backside like a lover's hand. He didn't get to the bar before a female hand reached out and patted his rump. Kinley had noticed how nicely his jeans fit, but had never thought about anyone else noticing, too. She wasn't sure how she felt about other women reacting to him like that. She saw

Jack jump backward at the tap on his backside, and laughed out loud. He may have to get used to that sort of thing.

At the bar, she saw him sandwich in between two women, both of whom vied for his attention. Kinley watched him tug his shirt cuff, shift from one foot to the other, and then actually jerk his head when a third woman shot him a wink and a smile. A sense of protection wrapped in a hint of jealousy told her Jack might need some help, but she shook off the feeling. He didn't need her help. *What a crazy thought*. Jack was a mature thirty-something year old. Sensible. Responsible. Practical. Now he had a whole new face, a whole new world was opening up. A world he never had but, she suspected, secretly wanted to experience. She'd let him. He deserved that after what he went through the past few months.

But the more she studied him, the less she really noticed any difference between pre-accident and major overhaul. Sure, he was leaner and toned, and the plastic surgeon had rearranged a few things, but Jack was really still Jack. His eyes were still as warm as a summer day, his expression still reflected intelligence, and he still displayed the gentle ways and great manners he'd always had.

But the women of the world didn't know any of that. Tons of women would hit on him now just because of the way he looked. The dilemma was, how long could she let them flaunt their wares and still protect him from the sharks while he sorted out the real from the deceptive as he experienced all that he should have years ago.

"Kinley, pay attention!"

Kinley had been so deep inside herself that she jumped when Judy touched her arm. She swiveled her head from watching Jack back to Judy and her date, Ron. "I am," was all she could think of in response.

"Where have you been hiding that hunk?" Judy asked, sidling closer to Ron.

Hunk? Kinley looked back at Jack. Yes, he was a hunk now, and women would surely notice him. The thought made her uneasy. She looked down at the table and picked up her drink. "If you mean Jack, you know I mentioned him plenty of times before." She sipped her cocktail. "What is this blue thing you ordered me, anyway?" She could taste the coconut and pineapple, but not much else.

"A Blue Hawaiian, and watch out. The rum can sneak up on you. But no changing the subject," Judy challenged. "You mentioned Jack fixed your computer, played video games with your brother, and was a whiz at home repairs, but what you didn't mention was that he was a god."

Ron laughed and threw his arm around Judy. "I'm right here and I can hear you."

She turned and patted his cheek. "You know you are adorable and I'm going home with you. Concentrate on that while I find out more about Kinley's friend." Judy turned back to Kinley and whispered, "If things don't go right with you and Jack…" She pointed to herself and grinned.

Kinley rolled her eyes. "Oh, come on now. Really? In front of Ron, no less?"

Waving a hand, Judy laughed. "Better in front of him than behind his back,"

"Still here," Ron said, his gaze narrowing.

"Still going home with you," Judy assured him, and then turned to Kinley. "But seriously now, Jack has the sexiest butt in the whole place. Did he have some rear-shaping lipo along with the plastic surgery?"

Kinley laughed. "No, rehab helped with the transformation. He had his knee replaced, and I suspect all the leg-lifts and squats are responsible for that transformation." She finished her drink and watched Jack over the rim of the glass. He still waited for his order, and more women had filled in around him.

"What's the four-one-one on him?" Judy asked, then sipped her cocktail. "Has he been married before or anything?"

"No. He's just a true blue nice guy."

Judy glanced over her shoulder at Jack. "With the way the ladies are honing in on him, he may not be available very much longer."

"If you're that curious about his love life, why don't you just ask him?"

"Because I don't want to hear *his* answer, I want to hear *yours*. You're the one hoarding the hunk. Maybe you'd like to tell me why."

Kinley felt her brow furrow. Had she been hoarding Jack? She straightened her shoulders. "He's very involved with his job and trying to get out of repair and into concept. Programming takes a lot of time, I'm told. He has this tough-guy boss, Rashesh, who works him around the clock. He does volunteer work at the elementary school, some computer thing, and until the accident, he had it set up to refurbish old computers for a couple of non-profits in the county."

"You make him sound like a saint," Judy sat back and crossed her arms across her chest. "Get to the good parts, and make it fast."

"Like what?"

"Like how does he kiss?"

Really? "How would I know that?" Kinley asked, tipping her glass to find more blue stuff.

"Somebody should." Judy looked back at the bar.

Jack had finally broken free and was on his way to the table, juggling the fresh drinks.

"I bet any of the women in this place would volunteer to assist with that little project, unless you've called dibs."

"I have not called dibs on anyone." Kinley felt her body stiffen at the remark. "But…"

"But what? Is he a free man or off the market?"

Kinley knew Judy was just trying to get a reaction. They'd been friends for years, and Judy used ploys like this when she wanted to trick Kinley into answering. She never had any trouble taking a joke or laughing at herself. Before, that was. But now everything was different. The accident had changed all that—the way she cared about Jack, thought about Jack, finally admitted to herself the way she felt about Jack made her feel vulnerable when she saw all the attention he received from the women in the place.

If she answered Judy aloud, she didn't know what it must have been, but Judy started laughing so whatever she said had worked. Suddenly whistles and shrieks from across the room made her look toward the commotion. She saw two more women join the crowd around Jack. His face was flushed, and he held up the drinks about shoulder height as he tried to dodge curvy bodies and make his way back to the table. But with every step, a different woman got in his way. Each made Jack acknowledge her in some way before she would let him pass.

When he finally made it back, he plunked down in his chair like a rock falling from a cliff. "Brutal in here tonight."

"Did you start a riot over there or something?" Kinley asked him, pointing across the room.

"No. Some of the ladies were just getting friendly." He pushed his chair closer to hers. "But if someone looks this way, act like you're with me so they stay away."

Kinley looked toward the bar. "Too late now. Not only are plenty of them looking, but one is coming this way."

The lady fast approaching was attractive, and Kinley watched her closely. Complete with long blond hair, tight jeans, and a white V-neck sweater, the woman left no doubt that Jack was in her sights. Judging from her bright red cheeks and unsteady walk, she had been drinking a little more than diet sodas. She was a fast one, too, because one minute she was weaving toward them, the next, she was leaning over the table offering Jack a pretty good view of her lungs. Two quarters sailed across the table.

"You forgot your change, sweet thing. I told the bartender I'd bring it to you." The woman honed in on Jack like radar until she narrowed her gaze as Kinley moved her chair closer to Jack's. She straightened and pointed to Kinley. "Oh. Are you with her?"

Jack swallowed hard a few times. He darted his gaze toward Kinley.

Flashing a wide smile, Kinley patted Jack's cheek. "I got this, honey." She looked at the women. "I can speak for myself," she said sweetly. "Not only am I with him, but we've been married ten years today."

The woman's mouth dropped open.

Kinley tipped her head toward Jack. "Darlin', why don't you show the nice lady the school pictures of our kids? I slipped them in your wallet when you got home from work." She swiveled her head to the woman. "We have five."

The blonde plastered a hand over the vee of her sweater. "Uh, no thanks." Then she rapidly left.

"Thanks for bringing over the change," Kinley called after her. "Milk money's due tomorrow." She turned back to Jack. "And that was only one of the forty-seven women here drooling over you. But no worries. I suspect when the word gets around you are married with five kids, they'll find someone else."

"Forty-seven?" His grin widened. "You actually counted?"

Kinley nodded. "Three left or you would have had a half-century's worth of oglers."

Judy and Ron laughed. "Kinley, you had a Blue Hawaiian, and he had 5-0. How appropriate!"

"How much *have* you had to drink?" Kinley asked her.

Judy continued laughing.

Jack's eyes widened as he glanced around the crowded room. "Is it always like this here?"

"Not usually. Tonight's all noisy and getting wilder by the minute for some reason," Kinley replied.

"Full moon maybe," Judy suggested.

Jack's gaze pinned her. "You're kidding, right?"

"Of course, I am kidding," Judy assured, flipping a hand. "It's just a figure of speech when the crazies come out in full force. Try to relax. You look like you're worried a vampire will pounce any second."

Shrugging, Jack grimaced. "I don't get out much."

"Apparently not," Judy agreed.

Jack turned to Kinley. "Just let me know when you want to leave."

From the tone of his voice, Kinley knew what he meant was *I want to leave now, if that's all right*. She really thought he would have a good time tonight. Women had been flirting almost from the time they had arrived, and he didn't have to do anything but show up. Wasn't that every guy's dream? And if that dream also included trying out a new face to check out the results, then having women drool all over him had to be incredibly reassuring.

Suddenly Kinley knew the problem. Jack was not used to this much attention. He didn't know how to act. A confident, self-assured attitude around the ladies was a practiced art, one learned in steps through dating trial and error. But Jack hadn't had many lessons like that. Being a guy, he wouldn't have admitted the weakness anyway before she dragged him out and tossed him into the cougars' and kittens' play area.

"I wouldn't mind going home now," she told him.

The way Jack leapt to his feet told her that she was right about everything.

Chapter Six

The night was dark and clear, the air as crisp as toast. Jack's new Honda Accord wasn't nearly as snappy as the little car he destroyed in the accident, but this one was bigger and safer. The night's silence folded over her. A white satin moon backlit the trees.

"I never thought I'd appreciate making a quick exit when out with you. Is happy hour always like that?"

"Sometimes days and nights are like that out in the world away from bits and bytes, and computer-generated avatars you control. The world is full of real people who have ideas of their own, not actions programmed by a gamer."

Jack laughed. "But you programmed in five kids in ten years. Come on."

Kinley tossed her head. "I know. Genius of me, wasn't it? Something had to scare off that cougar with her sights on you, and probably if I gave her a chance, her claws, too." She reached to lightly punch his arm. "Now that you look like you do, you'll need some quick lessons in self-defense if you expect to navigate the dating scene."

"I don't think I'm ready for that whole bar thing, do you?"

How could she possibly answer that question when all she could think about was how much she wanted to be the one dating him? Her feelings kept building daily, and she couldn't imagine sharing him with anyone else. But how could she deny him the experience of the hunt, of picking out an attractive woman in a crowded bar and going for it? From what he revealed about his dating experience, he never had much luck, and hadn't pursued the idea once he came to terms with his self-proclaimed nerdness. She believed every man needed the thrill of the chase, a field in which to sow wild oats, and the answer to all the "what ifs" rolling around bachelor heads before they committed to a relationship.

Relationship? She almost said the world out loud. She had no business thinking about any kind of a relationship with him right now. He'd been through quite the siege the last few months, and didn't need any more pressure. But could she deny the excitement that charged the air when they were together? Around Jack she felt like champagne, bubbling, building, ready to pop. That was the type of feeling she always wanted in a relationship. "You're still healing. Maybe for a while, you shouldn't overexert yourself." She silently chided herself for tap-dancing around his question.

"I feel fine."

When they passed under a streetlight, she noticed he was smiling. Beaming actually. "What?"

"What what?"

"You're grinning like the proverbial Cheshire cat."

Jack chuckled. "It's just that I felt different at the bar today."

"Different how?"

"I don't know. Different."

She knew. She shifted in her seat and rested her head against the headrest. "You felt a little sexy with all the attention you were getting, didn't you?"

"Did not," he snapped, his brows wrinkling in a frown.

"Not even when the blond patted your backside?"

Jack shot her a sidelong glance and nodded. "Well, maybe then. But it felt weird." He smiled. "Nice and weird."

"Then you better get used to weird, Handsome, because word's about to get out that Jack Reeves is a looker."

****

All too soon for Kinley, Jack pulled into her driveway. She'd been so used to being at his place during his recovery that she forgot she'd actually started out at her house this time. She rummaged through her purse for her keys. "You don't have to walk me to the door."

"I do. It's well past midnight, and I want to make sure you get in okay. Plus it's a little cold outside, and your coat is pretty lightweight."

"And I suppose if you had a cape, you'd take it off and give it to me."

Jack grinned. "Aren't super heroes supposed to do that?"

Kinley waggled her forefinger. "A super hero NEVER takes off his cape, Reeves. You, above all, should know that."

"Why? Because when you look at me you think once a geek, always a geek, even with a new face?"

Kinley was instantly sorry. Jack looked positively destroyed. That's not what she meant at all. "If Thor, cape included, is a geeky superhero, then sign me up." Confident her point was made, she didn't wait for him to get out and jog around the car to open her door, but simply opened the door herself. The night air hit her the minute her feet hit the ground. The day started out warm, but spring was a capricious season, and the cool air wrapped around her like a second skin. She moved her shoulders in an unintentional shiver.

With a grin that was all male, he walked to her side and threw an arm around her shoulders. "You didn't get your house key out of your purse while you were in the car, did you?"

"No."

"I see you didn't bother to turn on the porch light before we left, so you could see down into that suitcase you call a purse."

"Nope, I did not."

"Then, as a superhero, it is my duty to save the day and keep you warm while you hunt for your keys."

"This may take a while." She dipped her head and rummaged through the outside compartment on her handbag as the wind kicked up a notch. "You know, if you were as big as you used to be, I'd be a lot warmer."

"And if you carried a smaller handbag, I wouldn't have to play wind block." He pulled her close.

That's it. Find the keys quick. She was having a hard time holding onto righteous thoughts with Jack's arm around her. Her pulse raced as though she had just run a marathon. Her senses honed in on every detail about him—the slash of moonlight on his cheek, the way his hair ruffled away from his forehead in the wind. Just that quickly her female hormones ramped up, sending the age old man-woman awareness coursing through her veins. She had no problem recognizing that her hormones established her feelings had permanently moved from friend to wanting more. A lot more.

She hadn't been a teenager in a long time, but since this new madness for Jack showed up and knocked her on her keister, she sure felt like a lovesick freshman who had just been asked out by a senior. Every time she was with Jack, the feeling grew stronger, and every time the sensation shocked her.

Why she never before admitted he was more than just a friend, she didn't know. She knew the qualities she looked for in a guy. She wanted someone sensitive, caring, committed—all the adjectives she ever used when describing her perfect match—and each one of them were the same ones she used when describing Jack. But she'd never told him. She always thought she would get around to it someday, always thought there was time.

But since she almost lost him, she'd experienced a crazed madness set firmly in her heart that ramped up the urgency almost daily. She wanted to spirit him away, and hide him somewhere no one else could discover all his wonderful qualities now all wrapped up in an incredible physical appearance. But would that really be fair? To him? To her?

His packaging was about to open up a whole new world, which, by his own admission, he had never explored because of insecurity. Today he got a little taste of the kind of attention he would be getting, and she had no right to deny him experiencing more. Every guy deserved the chance to hunt a little and sow those proverbial wild oats. Actually, she wanted the guy she finally chose for a happily ever after to be way past that harvest.

When she looked up and at his face, everything around her stopped, and her thoughts scolded her. *Don't be an idiot and do something stupid. I kissed him every day at the hospital. If he wanted to do something more about the kisses, he had every chance. But he hadn't. I'd be crazy to trade his friendship for goopy-eyed delusions.*

"So if you want me to take off the air conditioner covers this weekend, I can," Jack said.

She forced herself to concentrate on his voice. "What?" *When did the conversation turn to air conditioner covers?*

"You shouldn't wait until the last minute to uncover those window units. Summer's coming. I could help you this weekend."

Help her? With her insanity, maybe. She dipped her head and concentrated on her purse so he couldn't see the chaos she knew would be in her eyes. "I've been meaning to get that done." She hoped her voice sounded normal. "But I couldn't seem to find time."

"Because you've been taking care of me?"

"And because the company gets busy in the spring. Everyone wants to spruce up and fix their places. The paperwork with quotes to process keeps on coming."

"I'll make you a deal," he said. "I'll uncover them this weekend if you make me dinner. Is it a date?"

A date? What kind of date? The friendly pop-over-any-time thing they've had up until now, or the kind she had started thinking about lately? Her heart began a rapid pitter-patter as she grappled with an answer. When she did finally find her keys on the bottom of her purse, she gripped them so tightly the key's teeth cut into her palm. A good thing because it brought her back to reality. "Found them," she declared, holding up the keys in front of her face.

And there they were. His incredible eyes. Not looking at the keys at all but focused firmly on her face.

"I was hoping you'd find those things sometime before daybreak," he teased.

"I found them. That's what counts." His eyes sparkled as his gaze roamed her face, and she swore she felt a gentle caress when the pleasant inspection focused on her lips. "Is that all?" he whispered before reaching out and tucking a strand of hair behind her ear. His fingertips trailed down the side of her neck like the airy touch of the softest feather. *Don't screw this up.* Decision made, she lowered the keys, rose up on tip-toes, put her hands on his shoulders, closed her eyes and kissed him.

Her lips barely touched his when she felt his body tense. She opened her eyes and let out a quick breath of air, wishing she could find a hole nearby into which she could jump. She backed down on her heels, her mind racing with an excuse or an apology. She'd go with whichever one came out of her mouth first. At this point, she didn't really care.

Then to her surprise, she felt Jack's arm go around her waist. His fingers sieved through her hair before his palm cupped her head. She had a moment to realize what was happening before his mouth came down onto her lips. The keys fell from her hand, and she didn't care if she ever found them again.

She kissed him every day while he was in the hospital and felt a connection. Ever since then, all she had to do was be around him to feel that connection grow stronger with each excuse she used to kiss him. But this time, the kiss went far beyond a connection. This kiss felt like magic. Emotion bounced back and forth between them as though it had been held in check for ages.

The groan that emerged from his throat sounded like every feeling trapped inside him for decades had broken free. His arms held her tighter, but his fingertips caressed her back as though she was made of glass. Her breath caught when the pressure of his lips deepened. Pressed against his chest, she could feel his heart thudding. As the kiss continued, she let go. Excitement swirled inside her with dizzying speed. She could not catch her breath or her common sense. Why had it taken something like a terrible accident for her to realize her true feelings for Jack? She never wanted this kiss to stop. He could kiss her into next week if he wanted to. Between the building feeling of happiness and the palpable excitement a nagging question rose. How could her perfect match have been right in front of her all this time, and she never knew it? She didn't have time to dwell on the answer as somewhere through the white noise inside her head, she heard his hoarse whisper and felt him lighten his kiss.

"Kin."

"Yes?" she whispered back.

"Oh hell," he said right before his mouth came back down on hers and he kissed her silly again.

Joyfully, she kissed him back. *This is the best day ever*.

"Kinley."

"What is it, Jack?" she whispered against his lips as her fingers tangled in his hair.

"Just a minute," he whispered back before kissing her again.

Her neck ached from the angle she held her head to

meet his kisses. Her toes ached from rising up to match his height. But she didn't care. Jack was kissing her, and she liked that he was.

"Kinley," he whispered her name again before his mouth lifted.

"Either tell me what you want, or shut up and kiss me some more, because obviously, you can't do both."

His fingers brushed the hair from her forehead before trailing a path to her shoulders and moving her gently away. She saw his eyes darken to a dream-filled haze. He was making it hard for her to think, but he said her name again, and she focused on his words.

"Kinley. I'm sorry. I must have lost my mind."

"And I lost mine." So what if they both lost their minds? This was Jack. Her Jack now. What was wrong with a little misplaced brain matter?

But he didn't say anything more, and she knew something was wrong. Very wrong. A frown creased his brow, and his gaze darted away from her face before he stepped back. He took a few short breaths before picking up her keys. "I'm sorry. I'm really sorry. I know you didn't expect something like that. We're friends, and I like that, so let's just forget about what just happened, and pretend it never did." He swallowed. "My fault. I should have never—" He stopped and rifled through her keys until he found the one to the front door. He held it out with his thumb and forefinger. "You need to get inside, and I need to go. I'll talk to you tomorrow."

She hoped he didn't see her hand shaking when she took the key ring. "Sure." She couldn't form any other words as she watched him nearly run to his car. She wanted him to stay, but found she refused to call out.

She watched him get into his car, back out of the driveway, and speed away. The moment for her to say anything disappeared like his vanishing tail lights.

For what felt like an eternity, she stood there. What had just happened? Her heart drummed with emotion and the sensation of wanting to keep kissing him hadn't left, but something didn't feel right. Her kisses should have made Jack feel wonderful, as wonderful as she felt. Instead, all he felt was sorry. Could she have been so wrong about everything?

Until the accident, she never focused much on the warm feelings she had for him. But though those terrible moments afterward, and over the ensuing weeks during which he endured surgery after surgery, days filled with enough rehab to make a linebacker wince, she knew her feelings had moved to a depth from which there was no return.

She wanted to talk to him about how she felt, had planned on doing just that. But the way Jack reacted tonight, telling him anything might just be a really bad idea. She wanted—no, needed—to share Jack's new life, but the mixed messages he sent out tonight made her wonder. Could she have been so wrong about thinking he had enjoyed kissing her as much as she enjoyed kissing him? Had she misread the emotions she thought she felt in his kiss? Or was there some other reason he didn't seem to want them to be anything more than the friends they were now?

Chapter Seven

The next morning Jack sat in the parking lot of Data Incorporated, sister company to Gaming International, and home to, among other things, the Nerd Herd, for the first time since his accident. For a while, he didn't move, trying instead to analyze his current problem, if it could be considered a problem.

Kinley.

Sweet, adorable, gorgeous Kinley.

Before the accident, every day seemed normal. Get up, work, and come home. Now, every day filled with an added dimension—get up, think about Kinley, write computer code, think about Kinley, go to bed, dream about Kinley. His hormones, the ones that used to be in a self-induced coma deeper than the sleep of Rip Van Winkle, were wide awake and ready to party.

At that thought, he gave his head a small shake. Maybe his first day back at work would put things into better perspective. Working from home, and having Kinley pop in to see him, while he recovered really screwed with his head. A little structure to his work day would definitely allow time to think more analytically. At least, he hoped so.

He got out of the car and crossed the lot toward his company's front door. As he answered a text message from Rashesh, he heard a wolf whistle followed by a very feminine voice calling out, "Hello, handsome." He ignored it, and kept on texting. Greetings like that had never been meant for him. When he finally looked up from his phone, he saw an ash blonde in a short black skirt and three-inch heels walking toward him. He nodded a polite greeting.

The instant their gazes locked, she winked and whistled again.

Instinctively, he looked around to see whose attention she was trying to catch, but no one else in the parking lot. The woman had actually wolf-whistled at him. *Holy cow!* That never happened before.

She stopped in front of him. "Sales or HR?"

Finger still poised above his phone's keyboard, he didn't understand at first what she meant. "Excuse me?"

The blonde whisked a stray lock of hair behind her ear.

He had to admit; the move was sexy.

"You must be either in sales or applying for a job, because you don't work here. I *know* I would have noticed you before."

When did women get so friendly? Then he remembered he no longer looked like the person who ran the place. "Neither."

"Pity. The hottie-list is a little light in there, and no doubt you'd be in the top three."

"Thanks, I think." The urge to sprint to the door filled him as soon as she stepped out of his way. He wanted to run, but instead walked slowly away. After all, he was CEO, and the role commanded a little decorum. But he did duck inside the main door as quickly as he could. Then head down, he made his way straight for the elevator.

He was stunned. Women flirting with him. The concept seemed as foreign as learning Mandarin Chinese might be. Ever since his new face emerged, he felt as though he'd been asleep and just awoke in another world where nothing made any sense.

No one treated him the same way they had before his transformation. People now made eye contact, smiled as he passed, or simply looked his way with something more on their faces than a polite stare. Outside he may look like a prince, but inside he was the same old frog he'd always had been. People gave him the impression they expected him to like the attention he was now getting, to welcome it even. But this particular side effect of the accident made him uncomfortable. He felt so confused. The women in the bar, the lady outside—they were strangers and were only interested in the window dressing. The admission might be a tad unfriendly, but they didn't matter all that much to him. But Kinley. She mattered. Did she expect him to feel different now, too?

"Excuse me," another female voice called out.

He glanced back but kept on walking.

"Sir, stop!"

Focusing on his phone, he almost made it to the elevator when he felt a hand grab his arm.

"Sir, you can't go upstairs without signing in and getting a visitor's pass."

What? Jack felt his eyebrows draw down in bewilderment. He had hired the security guard who was now attached to his arm with a vise grip, but she apparently had no idea who he was. He looked from her hand to her face and smiled. "Good morning, Linda. I'm sorry. I didn't know you were talking to me."

Linda's eyes widened, and she dropped her hand. "I'll be darned. Mr. Reeves?" She squinted and leaned forward. "Sounds like you, but you sure don't look like you. I heard you'd be coming back today, but I didn't know it would be with…" She bit back the rest of her words.

"It's okay. I had some surgery following the accident."

Linda put her hands on her hips and took a step backward. "I'll say. You definitely will need a new ID. Peggy. Come on over here," she shouted over Jack's shoulder.

The tapping of Peggy's approaching high heels on the tiled floor stopped just to Jack's right. "Can I help you with something, Linda?"

Linda stepped back and, with a flourish, pointed to Jack.

Peggy turned and gave a polite smile. "Can I help you?"

A nervous twitch had Jack tugging at his tie. He shot Linda an annoyed glance before turning fully to Peggy. "Good morning, Ms. Brooks."

She, too, leaned forward, her gaze scanning Jack's face. "Mr. Reeves?"

Jack nodded as a splash of red appeared on Peggy's face. "Yep, it's me."

"I am so sorry. We all knew you'd be back today, but…" Her face suddenly turned as red as it would if she had been sitting for hours on a beach in one hundred degree weather. "I mean you look great. Wonderful. Really good."

Smiling, Jack nodded. As soon as the elevator doors opened, he practically jumped inside. On the upstairs floors, he received basically the same response from Carol in Human Resources when he asked for a new ID and picture. Her gaze ran down his body, examining him from head to toe as thought she was eyeing a luxury car. When Barbara and Carrie from the Finance Department passed him in the hall, they turned a full circle watching him go by, making him feel as though he either forgot to zip or button something. On the way to his office, everyone stared as he passed by them. Some gave him a tentative nod; others began whispering to officemates. Now he knew how a new kid must feel on the first day of school. But instead of running to a bathroom stall for refuge, he'd find his solace in the corner office on the fifth floor.

Once there, he opened the door and instantly felt his body relax. The place looked like home, and felt just as good when he slid into his desk chair. Except for a small mound of papers on the desktop, nothing seemed to have changed. As he pulled the pile closer, he felt his nerves ease.

He flipped through the messages, noting they consisted mainly of welcome back cards and the handwritten greetings of well-wishers. He set aside the notes and turned on his laptop, eager to escape to the security of computer code. Binary numbers were predictable, like the sun rising in the east and setting in the west. Binaries were logical, simple, fast, and constant; the way his life had been right up until the day his face hit the car's windshield and changed things forever.

More mail and paper rested neatly stacked in his In-box. He rifled through the reports, analytics, and projections for the company, along with a stack of reports for the new batch of video games in various stages of pre-release, and began to feel more at home. *Good, this is exactly what I need right now.*

He pressed the Do-Not-Disturb function on the phone before ringing out to his administrative assistant, who gratefully wasn't at her desk when he walked in. "Cindy. I'm going DND. Take messages for a while. I have some catch-up to play in here." Without waiting for her reply, he grabbed the twelve-month projection report for War Zone III, logged onto the file he needed, and immersed himself in a world he felt a whole more comfortable inside.

He made it through two hours of uninterrupted work before lifting his gaze from the computer screen to the window. His reflection, still foreign to him, brought him back to reality. With that reality and the rhythm of a wild case of tachycardia, he saw Kinley's face race through his mind, spreading faster than a computer virus, replacing all common sense with a sense of her. He didn't even try to fight the way their kiss played through his memory in vivid detail.

Was it his imagination or his hope that a woman like Kinley—someone who had been way beyond his reach all his life—finally could actually be interested in him? The way she kissed him, eagerly, softly, happily, felt as though she enjoyed him. When he kissed her back, she enjoyed that, too. The thought drove him right out of his mind.

Since he met her, he'd been so careful around her. Afraid of rejection, he kept his demeanor light and friendly, and kept a lid on his hormones by sheer force of will. After all, a man had to do what a man had to do, even if sometime he got hurt doing it. She was an Alister, and he was a geek. She was excitement and laughter, and he was bits and bytes and computer code. He faced girl-boy reality in about the tenth grade, and nothing much had changed when it progressed to a man-woman thing. Guys like him were mind-numbing to most women, and from the few dates he'd had, he couldn't blame them. Heck, he'd bored himself sometimes. As a friend he didn't disappoint, but as anything more, he always failed. He didn't want to risk failing with Kinley. Doing so would literally kill him.

He stood and walked to the window, his mind firing like one of the ultra-automatic weapons in one of his computer games. He never dwelled much on the emotional stuff, never expected that he might have to. But all that changed when Kinley kissed him back.

The logical side of him basically understood why she reacted the way she had. The situation they found themselves in had been building for a while—the accident, his new face, the women in the bar. Women didn't like other women stepping into their space. Or so, he'd been told. He had no real experience in that arena. He suspected Kinley probably saw the way other women were looking at him now, and just reacted. The protective instinct. Like a mother protecting her young. That's what was happening. He had told her so many times about how benign and invisible he was to the opposite sex, that she probably just didn't want him to get hurt again. So she was just being a true friend. Plain and simple.

He had reacted, too. Kinley was beautiful and fun and perfect, and he responded like every other man probably did. But he was not every other man. He was her friend, and friends were not supposed to lie to each other. Unfortunately, he had been doing just that for a very long time.

The thought of his deceit felt like a shot to his heart with his duplicity as the bullet.

Friendship functioned hand in hand with trust, and Kinley's trust in him had been built on a lie. He had to come clean and tell her, fall on his knees when he did, and let her smack him with a rolled-up newspaper. Something. Anything. But he had to make the situation right. He had lived a double life for almost two years, and he couldn't do it much longer. Kinley deserved better. She deserved the truth.

"Jack!"

He spun at the familiar sound of Rashesh's voice.

"Welcome home."

Jack slipped back into his desk chair. "Thanks."

Rashesh sat opposite him. "I would have been here earlier, but I had a meeting with Tech. I knew you'd want to get an update on War Zone IV."

"No need. I uploaded the report, and just finished reading it. The projections look great. I see you've moved up the release date two months."

Rashesh nodded. "Strike while the iron's hot. WZIII has been the bomb. Sales are through the roof, and the advance orders on WZIV are three times as many as we thought they might be." He rifled through the file folder he brought with him. "The third-quarter sales on WZI and WZII are also more than expected." He slid the folder toward Jack. "We have a lot of gamers playing catch up."

"Still hard to believe in five short years, we've gone from garage start-up to this," Jack replied after reviewing the figures. "But that look on your face tells me that's not why you're here."

"The look on my face is probably in response to the look on yours." Rashesh shook his head. "I was just getting used to the mummy look. Now I'll take a while to get used to this one." He narrowed his eyes. "Sometimes, I forget it's you."

"It's still me."

"No, it's Jack 2.0"

"Ha. Ha." Jack spaced the forced laugh evenly for emphasis. "So, what's really up?"

"CEX."

"Crud." He tossed the file onto the desk. "The Computer Electronics Expo. I forgot all about it."

"I didn't." A smile crept across Rashesh's mouth. "Vegas, baby!"

Rashesh was talking. Jack saw his lips moving, but he didn't hear a word. All he heard was the screaming inside his head. *Holy cow. Holy Hell. Holy everything.* He couldn't go to Las Vegas. Not now. Maybe not ever. War Zone had a cult following, as though the video game had turned into the gaming version of "Twilight" and he was "Edward." Everyone—gamers, bloggers, reporters, editors—was trying to find out more about him. He was still amazed his interest in video gaming started the snowball rolling down the proverbial hill. Wasn't that what all successful people had been told? Write the book you want to read, make the movie you want to see, write code for the game you want to play. That's all he did. But as luck would have it, doing what he enjoyed moved beyond anything he could have ever imagined.

If he didn't figure out something fast, the Computer Electronics Expo might produce the snowball-rolling-downhill effect and engulf him. He could not continue to lead two lives after CEX. His face, his new face, would be plastered all over the convention center, and there would be no way to stop it.

"But that's not all."

Rashesh's voice somehow filtered inside Jack's brain and he turned his auditory sensors back on. Jack saw Rashesh pull out his tablet. Though he hadn't heard what Rashesh had been saying, he had a bad feeling about what was coming next.

"The Gamers and Lamers Blog has been doing some digging. For the last two months, the followers have been posting on the same subject."

"And the subject is?" His stomach churned with a premonition.

"You." Rashesh skated the tablet across the desk.

Jack stopped the tablet before it skidded onto the floor. A cold feeling ran down his spine when he read the post and saw the picture of his smashed car along with some pretty provocative questions—Where is Jack Reeves? Is he dead? Is he hiding? Has anyone seen him since this accident?

Chapter Eight

It was going to be one of those nights. Kinley decided as she watched Jack walk up her driveway. Shoulders hunched with hands in his pants pockets, he looked at the ground as he walked to the door. She'd seen this before. Many times. Every time, actually, when he hit a snag in one of his games or when he couldn't quite get the computer logic to click. Yes, by the looks of things, all was not well in the Kingdom of Nerdia.

But she knew a partial cure for what ailed him. Quickly, she tossed some chocolate chip cookies onto a plate and slid it into the microwave. A few beeps later and the rays were hitting cookie atoms, making them dance and warm. Chocolate chip cookies always made things better for Jack.

She opened her front door at the same moment the microwave beeped the all-done. "Hey," she said as he passed her, obviously following the scent of warm cookie. "Bad day in computer land?"

Still silent, he walked to the refrigerator and pulled out a fresh half-gallon of milk. He snapped off the top and started to raise it to his lips.

"Use a glass, you cretin."

He angled his head. "Excuse me?"

"A glass." She pointed to the cupboard. "Use a glass. We are not inside enemy territory in one of your games with nothing but a half-gallon of milk, and the hope our ammo will last as the enemy closes in. Be civilized." Looking perfectly distracted he didn't move, so she grabbed a glass and took the milk from his hand. "Did something happen at work?" she asked as she poured. "I felt a disturbance in the force." By the look on his face, she spotted that her attempt at humor fell flat.

"Did you hear something?" he asked, tapping his fingertips on the countertop.

"No. Should I have?" She lifted her chin and looked at his hand. "Are you nervous or upset?"

"I'm…stunned by all the attention, that's all?"

"You sure?"

He nodded and reached for a cookie.

She smacked his hand. "No food until you tell me why you look the way you do."

"My plastic surgeon got a bit carried away." He forced a grin.

"Jack, come on." She rolled her eyes. "That's not true. And besides, that's not what I mean. Your face is all squished up like you've smelled week-old fish." His turning into a hunk had its disadvantages. Before the accident, she could tell what was on his mind by the expression on his face, but now? She could see the lines on his furrowed brow and the angst in his eyes, but nothing more. Just how deeply the problem, whatever it was, bothered him, she couldn't tell. "What's wrong?"

"It's work."

She should have known. His first day back, and Rashesh probably gave him fits over the work piling up on his desk. "What did that bully of a boss do?"

"Nothing. It's Monday."

"Yes, and tomorrow is Tuesday."

"No, I mean it's Monday. Only Monday." He slumped. "The receptionist practically threw herself in front of the door when she thought I was crashing the floor, but then after I got that straightened out, the next time she passed me in the hall, she made sure she caught my eye. She never did that before. And people kept coming around looking at me. Guys said I am about to start getting extremely lucky, and some of the ladies slipped me their phone numbers. And it's only Monday," he repeated with a groan.

"Oh," Kinley mumbled.

"I am seriously thinking of asking the plastic surgeon for my old face back."

Kinley shook her head. "I don't think that'll happen. You have to get used to looking wonderful."

"If you say so, but wonderful or not, I have a problem, and I would appreciate your advice."

Kinley tried to read the expression on his new face, but again failed. "You're serious."

"I am."

New face or old face, the turmoil in his eyes was easy for her to see. "Okay, I'm listening."

"Everyone, especially women, is treating me differently now. When I was walking to my car tonight, I heard a couple of college girls whistle at me. I didn't know what to do, so I waved. Then one of them gave me her business card. I didn't know what to say, so I said 'thanks'." He blew out a long breath of air and shook his head. "What a jerk I am."

She smacked her hand on the table. "You are not a jerk."

"I am. I mean, I like women and women like me,

as a hands-off friend kind-of-guy. That's my reality. But this man-woman thing that's happening now, in that, I'm a jerk. Always have been."

"Cut it out, Jack. Stop being so hard on yourself. Maybe the women you picked over the years have been the jerks."

"I'm just being realistic. I got a new face, and women are finally looking at me the way I've always hoped they would. But that only happened because I don't look like me. But I am me." He patted his chest. "Inside, I am the same. A change on my face doesn't automatically make me a stud or someone cool who knows what is supposed to happen next. I was nothing more than furniture to them before I got this new face, but now they look at me like I'm lunch."

She wanted to respond, but her heart pounded, really pounded. She tried but couldn't even imagine how Jack must be feeling. If she heard a direct request for advice, she'd gladly give it. Unfortunately, she couldn't help but feel no matter what she said would only dig herself a deeper hole.

"Anyway," Jack continued, sinking into one of the chairs in the living room. "You must have had a million guys flirt with you since you turned ten."

"That would only be the pedophiles," she cut in, hoping to make him smile.

"Okay, then since you turned fifteen." He hunched forward and rested his forearms on his knees. "I was hoping you could tell me what to do when women flirt with me. Tell me what they expect."

The statement hit hard and Kinley's heart beat faster. Rushing blood made her feel light headed. Now what? Apparently, he had already put their kisses behind him, was getting ready to move forward in the dating game, and wanted her to teach him how to play it. "You want me to help you flirt?"

"Sort of, kind of. More like help me maneuver through this mine field I walked into."

"Okay." She swallowed the awkwardness she felt. "I can do that. But every situation is different. There's no how-to script written. It's more improv."

Jack closed his eyes and shook his head, "Then I'm doomed."

"No, you're not. You're just a rookie. All you need is a little practice."

"Do you have a playbook, coach? I think I need one."

She wrinkled her nose. "Cute."

He smiled and pointed at her with a "gotcha" gesture.

"I don't have a plan, yet, but for starters, let's try to establish a no-hussy zone. Like a home base where you can hole up and get away from it all."

"That would be great. Can I get a sign like that at the office supply store?" He closed one eye and held up his hands like a director would frame a shot. "I'd love to put one on the office door."

Huh? Kinley furrowed her brow. "You have an office now?"

Jack shot his eyes wide. "Ah...I'm using one for a while."

"Then how about I stop by around lunch tomorrow, and let all the ladies at work see you with me?"

"And that will...?"

"You really are a rookie, Reeves. The office rumor mill will churn out an APB about us as a couple, thereby buying you some time. What have you got to lose?"

"Maybe there's a book or something I can read." He pulled out his phone. "Or may someone wrote an app for dealing with situations like this."

"Not yet." She took the phone from him, rather than risking having him find one. She liked the idea of being his pretend girlfriend, if only for practice until she could become the real thing. "Maybe I should write one."

"As brilliant as you are, you still couldn't. Too many variables, not the least of which is motive and opportunity."

"Sounds like a murder case."

"Believe me, the two parallel at times." Watching the play of emotion on Jack's face, Kinley wondered about her own motive. Was she as pure in her desire to make sure Jack got the attention he never had, or would she be at his side twenty-four-seven so she could make sure no one else staked a claim? There were no quick answers so she buried the question for now.

She sat next to him, and took him by the shoulders. "How you react to a lady's motives is all in the body language." She shook him. "Relax. Loosen up. Right now, your body language is transmitting the keep-off signal."

"The keep-off signal?" His gaze darted back and forth, and his lips pressed into a thin line.

Kinley nodded and let go of his shoulders. "You're stiff, rigid. If you want to feel comfortable in any situation, you need to send out friendly body language saying you like people and want to get to know them."

His brow furrowed. "But wouldn't that invite the

hussy-ladies, too?"

"I said friendly, not come on down and party. You have to learn the difference between the two if you want to survive."

Jack crossed his arms in front of him. "Isn't it easier to just tell them?"

Fighting back a smile, she looked him up and down, "Do you know what you're telling them now?"

He lowered his arms. "Apparently not hello?"

"More like—what are you looking at?"

Jack slumped his shoulders. "I'm hopeless."

"You are not. You just need some work." She bit down on her lip. "But with that new face, you also have to be careful you don't send out the come-and-get-me signal."

"Come and get me?" The furrow in his brow deepened.

She nodded. "It's all in the body language."

He looked down and swept his hand down his length. "I don't think I act any different."

"You probably can't. You are a naturally friendly person. But seeing your new look, some women will take that friendly stuff as meaning something more."

"I don't get it."

"I know." She let her shoulders drop. "We have to practice. A lot." She pressed her lips together, thinking. "Listen. Say you are having lunch one day and notice the lady at the next table has dropped her napkin. You get up from your chair, go over to her, pick up the napkin, and hand it back. She smiles, you smile. Then you return to your table."

"I was being polite. I've done that."

"I hate to break it to you, stud, but you just told

that lady you are available." She saw Jack's eyes first widen and then narrow under drawn-down brows.

"I did not."

Kinley nodded. "I'm guessing you didn't notice that when she took the napkin, she let her hand linger on yours, or that when she smiled, she focused her gaze on your lips."

"That didn't happen."

Kinley held up her hand. "Then you walked back to your seat, and she watched every part of your body move."

"If I was walking away, how could I notice something like that?" He stopped and cocked his head. "Wait a minute, none of that happened."

"Not yet. But it will, and you have to understand that now those friendly signals of yours mean something totally different than they used to mean."

He drew down his brows and shook his head. "I don't play games. I don't understand women enough to even try."

"You better start. Think of talking to the ladies as though they were in one of your video games. Don't be Jack. Be your avatar. Be Dakota." She shrugged. "Dating can be like another reality anyway."

"No way, Kin. In video games, I know the rules and the characters. You told me, no rules exist out in the dating world, and I don't even know enough to fake it." Shaking his head, he threw up his hands. "This is hopeless."

"Trust me. I promise if we practice a little role playing, I can show you how to read the signals, and how to give off a few of your own." Excitement at the possibilities swirled in her mind, and she managed to contain the smile that threatened to break out on her face. "Like one day I'll be the new office girl, the next time I'll be the nasty vixen, and another time, the lady on the prowl."

"And what do I do?"

"You just respond, and I'll help you understand what your response means. Eventually, you'll learn to read what the women want, and let them know how you feel about it, all without words." She saw skepticism race across his face. "We'll work on it. Don't worry." She shooed him into the kitchen and gave him half of the cookies she'd made. "Now go home and get some rest. Class begins in the morning."

She got a kiss as a thank you. A quick brotherly smack on the cheek wrapped in a grin. But for one long moment, he rested his gaze on her face, seeming to study her with enough raw emotion to make her heartbeat rise. Then he popped a cookie in his mouth and left.

She folded her arms across her chest, leaned back on the door, and slowly smacked the back of her head against it a few times. Was she totally insane? What in the world made her offer to school Jack in the art of dating? Jack. Her Jack. The Jack who, just the day before, kissed her and held her as though she was the woman he wanted to be with more than anyone else in the world.

Until the accident, Jack's self-deprecating put-down's had always been humorous or intended to be that way. But now, she realized he seriously lacked confidence in himself as a man. She knew she couldn't continue to allow him to feel that inadequate. She cared too much. To deny him the exploration of what he'd hardly experienced as a man, an attractive, desirable man, was equally as reprehensible.

One last time, she smacked her head and then locked the door. She turned off the lights and started up the stairs for bed, trying to decide what she wanted and needed from their relationship. She suggested the teacher-student idea to help him ease into dating because she wanted to make sure in his inexperience, he didn't do something he'd later regret. A pang of guilt raced through her, and she had to admit that wasn't the entire reason.

Now the teacher-student concept felt more like a test, rather than a coaching. She'd drawn a line in the sand—maybe to test him and test herself, as well.

On which side would they both land?

Chapter Nine

Jack looked at the man reflected back on the gray computer screen on the desk in his office. What in the world was he supposed to do with that man? The inside had not changed. The outside…well…he didn't know that person. Might as well be an avatar he created for any video game. Would he be expected to embrace an image he didn't know, or could he still be the person he knew was trapped inside new packaging?

He hit a series of keystrokes, and the image disappeared as the monitor came to life. A few entries later, and the task felt familiar and safe once again. The grids and codes didn't care how he looked. He was needed with no questions asked.

Back to the door, he didn't turn when he heard someone come into the office. When he was busy creating a new video game, he could ignore a hurricane.

"Package for you," a female voice said after a while.

Jack waved over his head. "Put it on the desk." He waited but did not hear the woman leave. He continued to punch in code. "Thanks," he called out. Still, no movement. A throaty chuckle whispered in the air followed by sultry perfume that attacked his nostrils.

"They told me in the mailroom that you were dedicated, hon," the woman said.

He didn't recognize the voice, and hated the

perfume, but the 'hon' made him snap up his head. No one had ever called him that before. Heck, as far as he knew, he never expected to hear the expression in his presence unless it came from a screen when he was watching some chick-flick.

He turned, intending to make eye contact with the women, but his gaze never got to her face. When he swiveled his chair, he found himself two inches away from her chest. Immediately, some primal instinct took instant hold, and he couldn't look away.

There were breasts, and then there were *breasts.* These two were the latter. A button tried to contain these two particular breasts inside thin shirt fabric but failed miserably. No man breathing could ignore what was being presented. Long platinum blond hair cascading over female shoulders framed enough cleavage to turn any man into a puddle of sweat. Not to mention the owner of the two particularly spectacular body parts did not mind breaking every part of the office dress code that applied to decency.

Being a grown mature man he knew he should turn away, look at anything else in the room, but he also knew in order to do that he would probably have to reach up and pluck out his eyes. Some sort of stupor fell over him. He couldn't move; he couldn't look away.

"I heard you were shy." The woman kicked off her stilettos and moved to the well-worn brown leather office couch. Her skirt jacked higher across her thighs when she sat and crossed her slim legs. She patted the sofa cushions. "Come. Sit."

Jack finally came to his senses and stood. "What are you doing?"

"I'm Monica. I'm new and getting to know

people."

"I'm sorry, Ms.?"

"Monica," she corrected, rising. "Just Monica." She walked toward him, her hips in an animated sway.

Blood pounded in his ears, and he backed up. "Monica, you need a class on harassment."

She laughed, and brushed the hair from her eye with her right hand. "Giving or receiving?" She circled his desk.

He tried to keep it between them. It didn't work.

The strong perfume got closer then pounced.

A hundred or so pounds wrapped in soft curves suddenly came at him like a shot. He had to choose fast—hang on to her, or let her bounce on the floor. She may not be a lady in the strictest sense of the word, but he was still a gentleman. He caught her when she jumped, and the impact took his breath away. Not because of her weight, but because of the way she curled her legs around him when she slammed against his body. He swayed and fell back into his desk chair.

She settled herself onto his lap. Two red polished fingers walked their way up his chest and then wound around his neck. "I guess this could be sexual harassment, but only if unwelcomed."

Lips the color of dark red roses hovered just above his. *Okay. This is bad. Very bad.* As the hair at the back of his neck twirled around her forefinger, he found he could not move. His heart thundered and threatened to explode in his chest. Even hit with a Taser, he expected he would react faster. Is this what women did to guys? He never knew. How could he?

"Want to get to know me better?"

He heard her ask somewhere from inside the white

noise that occupied his brain. *Yes!* The purely male side of him shouted.

No! Reality shouted back. *This chick is a lawsuit waiting to happen. Get her off me, out of the office, and off the payroll as soon as possible.* "Lord help me," Jack whispered.

And help came.

The office door banged open. "Jack, how about we—"

Jack recognized Kinley's voice, but it sounded like someone whispering at the same time a train whistle blew, and he was on the tracks with no time to react before the train hit. He craned his neck around the woman in his lap and spotted her.

With a lethal calm that chilled the room, Kinley walked to Jack's desk and extended her hand. "I'm Kinley. Jack's girlfriend."

With a gasp, Monica slammed her stocking feet to the floor. She glanced back at Jack as she took Kinley's hand. "Maybe not for too much longer."

Jack suddenly remembered Kinley's body language lecture. At this moment, Kinley looked like a trained Navy Seal on a mission.

"No such luck, sweetheart," she said, not letting go of Monica's hand until they both reached the office door. "Bye," she called out sweetly before shoving Monica through it. She turned back, her gaze settling on the discarded high heels lying on the office floor. Without a word, she scooped them up, opened the door, and tossed them through the opening. Then she stood with her arms crossed. "Now, that's a high-potency package."

Jack couldn't stop his mind from whirling like a

tornado. "Are all women like that?"

"Like what? Charlotte, the Harlot?"

"Monica." He knew he shouldn't have said it almost at the same time he did.

"Oh, you two are on a first-name basis already?"

He saw Kinley's face cloud like an incoming thunderstorm. "She told me her name right before she…" *Shut up, Jack. When in a hole, stop digging.* He saw lightning flash in Kinley's eyes.

"What was she doing on your lap?" She jammed her hands on her hips.

"I was working on the computer, and I thought the guy from the mailroom came in to deliver something. Before I knew what was happening, I had…"

"A lapful of curvy backside." Kinley finished for him. "I come here for lunch and I find you trying out the proverbial casting couch. What on earth were you thinking?" Shaking her head, she raised both hands. "Never mind, don't tell me."

Jack held up his hands in a don't-shoot gesture. "I don't know, Kin." He pointed to the door. "That never happened to me before. I was ambushed. What was I supposed to do?"

Kinley opened her mouth to respond and then stopped. She pointed. "You're right. You don't know what to do. You wouldn't. But you better learn fast. There's a whole lot more of them out there, waiting." She took his hand and led him back to the couch. "Sit. I came here for lunch, but it appears we need school instead."

"School? What kind of school?" *This doesn't sound good.*

"Not like classroom-and-textbook school. More

like the kind of schooling guys do over beers or while smoking in the boy's room."

The apprehension did not subside. "Girls know about that?"

"We had our own love lessons, so pay attention. Women on the prowl can be divided into three basic types. These types really don't change much through time, although the names vary. You just got up close and personal with Type A. A diverse set of names apply to Type A, but they all mean the same thing. In ancient times, girls like her were either stoned to death by righteous mobs, or else, they earned a lot of money." She shook her head. "From the look of her clothes, I could have used a big rock to throw when I walked in on you."

Jack laughed. "I get the picture."

"Then on the other side of the spectrum is the Forbidden Fruit. Type B. The pure virginal type. You have to work your butt off to even get a kiss from one of those types. Definitely a problem for guys who are, shall we say, inexperienced."

Jack furrowed his brow. "Why? I would think the first one would be more dangerous."

Kinley grabbed Jack by both shoulders. "Comments like that are precisely why you need my help. Tess Pureheart will scar you for life, if you get past first base. The guilt she will lay on you will have you down on one knee proposing for staining her lily-white virtue, even though you probably never slid into home plate. So be careful with that one. Be polite. Smile. Nod." She wagged her finger before his face. "But no touchie, unless you plan on asking her daddy for her hand."

"Gotcha." He nodded. "What's number three?"

"The Tweener. The most dangerous one of all. She is capable of moving back and forth between Type A and Type B, depending on whether or not she likes the guy she's with."

"Sounds complicated."

"And dangerous."

"How do you know what to do with the Tweener then?"

"You have to read the signals."

His lips tightened to a thin line. "And no one has made an app for identifying all the types with their signals either?"

"There will never be an app for that."

"Then I'm doomed."

"Not doomed, just untrained. Right now, you're just in first grade, Jack. We have a long way to go before you graduate into the wild world of dating."

"So before I get my dating diploma, how do I recognize the dreaded Type C? Do you guys carry a card or something?"

Her chuckle whispered into the air. "Isn't it just like a techno-geek to want a flowchart?" She sat beside him and arched an arm around his neck. Her fingers moved slowly across his neck. "But let's first go over what we learned from what happened just now," she whispered into his ear.

Jack couldn't concentrate. Not because he was in shock but this time because having Kinley next to him like this felt so good—her hip pressing against his, her light perfume filling every sense he owned, her soft voice playing havoc with his hormones. For a second, a heart-stopping second, he actually forgot that she had promised to help him read the feminine signs. Despite how much he liked what she was doing, he knew she was obviously playing a part, delving into feminine flirting while feeling safe because he was the same old nerdy guy who needed serious help, no matter how he looked.

He'd play it cool. Read the signals she was sending, and let her know he understood. But what he couldn't quite get under control was his thundering heart and building hormone level. Right now, he didn't feel like a nerd. Instead, he felt like a guy who just ran into the woman he'd always dreamed about, but knew he could never have in his life. Just like always.

"So what have you learned?" she asked before giving him a quick kiss on the cheek.

"That I should keep my office door open?"

"Anything else?" Her second kiss moved closer to his mouth.

"Some women don't like to take 'no' for an answer."

"And?" She kept on kissing him.

He had no more answers, but turned into her kiss. His pulse raced and his hormones soared like a climbing jet, rising and spinning, and just as hot. He pulled her to him, his hands stroking her back, his fingers sieving through her hair. He heard her gasp and then take in another breath of air before coming back for another kiss. Then another and another.

For long seconds, he enjoyed more of what she was giving before his annoying conscience shouted warning words of caution, reminding him Kinley was doing her job, one he agreed to let her do. Maybe this teacher-student thing loosened up a few inhibitions, but that didn't mean she felt anything for him. He had to try to remember that nothing about what was happening was real.

That's when he snapped off the volume and pulled the plug. He didn't want to listen to anything the voice of reason had to say, didn't want to think about sensibility at all. All he wanted was to keep on kissing Kinley. All this latent emotion he never thought he had kicked up, like an explosion ready to happen, and Kinley was the flame. Kinley was the power source for everything he was finally feeling, and he wanted to see what would happen next. But suddenly, the kissing stopped.

"Pop quiz," Kinley said, pushing back from him. "What signals am I giving you right now?"

"Pretty good ones." Grinning, he reached for her.

She stood and walked away. "Get serious, Reeves."

"I'm trying to."

"We need to talk about Monica, your lap, and how to read signals that say something like that is about to happen before someone like her gets farther along than she did."

"If there were signals, I never saw them." *But I see yours.* She stood close enough for him to kiss, but he held on and tucked the urge away.

Her mouth formed a thin, straight line. "You have signals, too. Possibly you've been emanating that you are asking for it."

"Asking for it? Come on, Kin, you know me better than that." He stood and raised his hands. "Never in a million years would I take advantage of anyone. Especially not at work."

"Let's face it. You've turned into a hunk, and

women are noticing."

Jack saw humor tinge her smile although her eyes reflected seriousness. "So you're saying my looks matter the most."

"No. Yes." Shaking her head, Kinley sighed. "Looks matter. We all know that. But it's how we *look* that sends out the message to other people."

He made sure he sat closer this time. "You lost me."

This time, her sigh was louder. "Okay. It's like in your video games. The avatar tries to assess his opponent by watching movements and reactions. Is this guy a good guy or a bad guy? Can I trust him? Can we communicate? It's the body language that helps you decide whether to shoot or not."

"Okay. I get you now."

"But when a women pats a guy's butt just like what happened to you in the restaurant, or when a lady"—she wrinkled her nose—"and I use the term extremely loosely in this case, suddenly comes on to you like Monica did, she isn't always reacting to a guy because he looks like Brad Pitt. Sometimes, the ladies are in hot pursuit because the guy gave the 'hello, baby, lookee here' signal in the way he walks or the way he acts." She hesitated, her gaze on his face. "You have a habit of putting yourself down and calling yourself a nerd, and you do it all with a smile that is so endearing. To laugh at yourself and come across as someone a woman can talk to and feel safe with is rare these days. Did you ever stop to think for one minute that some women may actually find that trait pretty darn attractive?"

Jack frowned. "I've never really thought one way or another about how anyone saw me since I left college."

"Well, you better start. The way you walk and move sends out messages to other people, and tells them a little about who you are. Couple that with the fact you look a lot like Chris Hemsworth."

"I do?"

"A little."

He smiled. "You like Thor?"

"I'm a fan," she admitted.

"I could get into swinging a big hammer and saving the world."

And I could get into seeing you in a cape with your hair flowing in the wind. She shook off the thought. "Pay attention and stop distracting me. As I was saying, the game has changed since you were a teenager, Jack. Actually, the dating game is in constant flux. You may just find you have women lining up outside your office door. How would your boss like that?" Kinley cocked her hip when Jack's expression fell. "You are not processing any of this, are you?"

He was processing all right. The mention of his 'boss' hit him in the gut, reminding him of the two-year ongoing lie he was still living. The longer he procrastinated, the worse the situation became. When he finally got enough nerve to confess to Kinley, he knew nothing would ever be the same as it was before he went out for Chinese, and came back with a new face. How could his life ever be the same now?

The day of the accident, his plan was to tell her over dinner that he had been breaking one of the really important Commandments for two years. Which one was it? The sixth? Seventh? Maybe he should have paid more attention in Sunday school, but he knew the words were thou shalt not something. No matter which one he crushed on a daily basis, his predicament would be worse once he confessed. Kinley would be angry but, before the accident, he'd been fairly confident he could talk her into forgiving him. Then proverbial hell broke loose, and the moment for soul-baring passed, along with all the other moments for confession he'd ignored. Still wrestling with guilt, somewhere inside his self-made hell, he heard Kinley's voice.

"Forget talking, just watch." She walked to the door, turned then walked toward him with eyes downcast and shoulders drooped, shuffling invisible papers from hand to hand. She met his gaze for a second and then looked away. "Hello," she said in a voice no louder than a whisper and bit her lip. "I'm from the mail room. I need a signature for this." She held out the pretend papers, kept looking from the mail in her hand to him then she squared her shoulders. "Who did you see?"

"Someone who would rather be anywhere else but talking to me."

"Good. Now, one more time." She walked back to the door. This time when she swung around and approached, she stood tall, shoulders back, gaze on his face. She smiled. "Hi, there," she said in a firm tone when she got to the desk and extended her hand. "I'm Kinley from the mail room. I need you to sign for this." Her gaze held his, and she dropped her hand slowly after the greeting as her smile grew. "Do you see what I'm trying to show you?" she asked after a few moments. "Same person. Nothing different about me physically, but the way I walked and acted sent out different messages. The first example was a hesitant, somewhat friendly person, but also a very insecure person. My body language said 'you can talk to me but don't get too close.' The second example was someone confident, and a little flirty. At lot like you."

A break-through? "You think I'm flirty?"

"You're confident. That makes you flirty."

"I don't flirt with women. I don't know how."

"Oh, but you do," Kinley corrected. "A man can flirt without realizing it."

Really? He threw up his hands. "This woman-reading thing is hard. As you said, Teach, I am still in the first grade."

Kinley smiled. "Before the accident, you purposely gave off a lot of 'keep away' vibes. But now, you smile more, your voice has more happy in it."

"And now I'm doing a 'lookee here'?"

She nodded. "What I'm suggesting is maybe you didn't change because you got a new face and lost some weight, maybe you changed because you are happier now and feel like you finally can fit in."

Jack thought about what she said for a moment before answering. "I don't think so."

"It doesn't matter, Jack. Whether you're giving off all those wonderful, confident, hunky signals on purpose or by accident isn't important. You need to remember that when a guy like you smiles, and is nice to a woman, she is programmed by nature to translate that signal into 'he's interested'. Maybe Monica picked up on something like that when you acknowledged her in the hall one day, or when you brought a batch of mail to the mailroom."

"I never even spoke to her before today."

"Okay, bad example." She tapped her forefinger on

her lips. "This is what I'm trying to say. Women like Monica are shallow. They only like the packaging. You need to find a real woman, one who cares about you. Remember when the lights go out, we all look the same, and the heart and soul of a person is all that really matters."

Your heart and soul always mattered. "Maybe I already found someone with those qualities."

Kinley laughed. "Who? Monica?"

"No, you."

"Stop joking, Jack."

"I'm not laughing," he responded.

Kinley wrinkled her nose. "I get it. You're in acting mode." She looked at her watch. "Darn. Gotta go. My lunch hour is over, and you once again owe me something to eat."

"Dinner tonight?"

"Pick me up at seven." She started to walk away but turned back. "I hope you were paying attention, because this was just the first lesson of many more to come. Tonight, I want a full report on what happens around here this afternoon." At the office door, she stopped. "This is nice. Did you get promoted from Fix-It Guy to Office-Guy?"

"No." He almost choked on the word. "I get to take it easy for a few weeks before I go back out in the Nerdmobile."

"Probably a good idea. Don't be late tonight, Reeves. I envision a candy bar in my future as lunch so that leaves a lot of room for dinner." She blew him a noisy kiss, and then she was gone.

Jack's smile faded. He didn't need a lesson to read those signals. That was a 'goodbye, see you later friend', exit if he ever saw one, not 'I can't wait to see you later, lover'.

He stood and rolled his head from side to side to loosen the tension. He had about twenty minutes before a hastily called board meeting, and he needed every minute to get his mind back on business. But his mind wouldn't cooperate. All he could think about was Kinley.

He knew things had changed for them. Now, her expression was vulnerable in a yearning kind of way. Her kisses, which started out playful in the hospital, turned into something intense and hungry when they both let down their guard.

As he saw it, he was the problem. He enjoyed the way she looked at him like he was sexy and attractive. He couldn't deny that. But his new face and body wouldn't mean a thing when she found out that fix-it guy who drove the nerdmobile actually could slap down enough cash to buy a *Lamborghini Testarosa*. When the lights went out maybe his new face wouldn't matter, but he would still be a liar.

Chapter Ten

By the time Jack got his mind back on work, he had a pile of messages needing his attention; five from Rashesh alone, and all in the last fifteen minutes. *Must be important.*

"Where's the fire?" Jack asked when Rashesh came into the room.

Rashesh said nothing but placed his knuckles on the desk and leaned forward. For a moment he stood there staring. Then he blinked.

"That's my cue," Jack said. "What's up?"

"You asked where the fire was when I came in."

"I did."

"And I told you yesterday that I was trying to put out fires."

He drew down his brows. "What are you telling me?"

Rashes pointed to the laptop on Jack's desk. "The firestorms are all in there, and they are all out of control." He straightened and shifted to the balls of his feet.

The glimmer of sweat beading Rashesh's brow began to make Jack edgy. "Sit down and…" he paused. "Tell me."

"I am guessing you haven't been watching the stock lately?"

Jack shook his head. "Can't say that I have, or ever

did for that matter. Besides, the market's a mess. It's up…it's down. Who knows how long before it stabilizes? The company will survive."

"The IPO is ready to roll out. You know what happens to a lot of internet start-ups when they first rolled out."

"Nothing like that will happen to Games," Jack drummed his fingers on the desk. "And if it does, the hiccup will work itself out. The company is solid."

"Maybe so. "

Jack noticed the sober expression on Rashesh's face had not changed. "What else?"

"The gaming blogs. Have you read any, say within the last week or so?"

"No." Jack dragged out the word like a question.

"Maybe you should have. A couple of the most ardent bloggers almost have you all figured out. GameSpot and TalkingTech have actually joined forces and put out a time line on your activities. The blogs have invited members to fill in the blanks. You know how unrelenting techies are. Someone will get into both the hospital and police records, link them up, and put a transformation story together. Can't be stopped. The rebooted Jack Reeves is poised to be outed all across the internet."

No! Jack felt tiny droplets of sweat break out on his forehead. "How much time do you think I have?"

Rashesh shook his head. "As smart as some of the gamers are, maybe only nanoseconds. Once the truth, the whole truth, and nothing but the truth, hits the internet, word will spread faster than light speed. If the story and a video show up on some internet video site, and it will, I bet the record for views will crumble."

"You're exaggerating. I am not that interesting. The story on the guy who shot up his daughter's laptop for her internet ranting is exciting. Me." He shrugged. "Not so much."

"If I exaggerate, then you underestimate." Rashesh rocked back on his heels. "A multi-millionaire who nearly gets killed going out for Chinese is a story. Add to that, this particular multi-millionaire now looks like a movie star, and that's an internet sensation."

"Doubt it." *I don't need or want the attention that story will bring me.*

"Don't." Rashesh leaned over, and a few clicks later, an entertainment news site was up on Jack's laptop. "Look what is trending. A celebrity unfriends other celebrity on some internet social site, and that's news. An actress admits she was once slightly overweight, that's news. Look here…" He pointed to the last entry. "This actress says she doesn't believe in deodorant, and that's news too. What do you think will happen when before and after pictures of you are posted?" Rashesh shook his head. "You can't stop the story from happening. It's only a matter of time."

Jack thought for a moment. "The luxury of my waiting for the right moment to tell Kinley the truth about me is over. That is a huge problem."

"You have two huge problems, Jack," Rashesh paced the length of the office. "The Trustee Board is really unhappy with some of the stock projections, and they are waiting. You'll have to figure out later how to get yourself out of the hole you steadily dug for the past two years. Right now, as Ricky Ricardo would say, 'we have some 'splaining to do, Lucy'."

****

Kinley glanced at the clock, Jack would be picking her up for dinner in about twenty minutes, and she needed every bit of the time to finish getting ready. She looked in the full-length mirror that leaned against the wall in her bedroom. No, this look would never do. Black dress, black stockings, three-inch heels. She looked like a call girl. A hot call girl maybe, but definitely not the tone she wanted to set tonight.

As she ripped clothes out of her closet, she wondered if maybe her original outfit choice had something to do with the co-worker on Jack's lap earlier. Unconsciously perhaps she wanted to recreate the mood, and end up on his lap by the end of the night. No, that wasn't right. Her mind needed to stay on helping Jack get used to his new look, not trying to seduce him. At least, not yet. He needed time and space to get comfortable in his new skin.

She changed into pants and a clingy tunic top, still angry at herself for suggesting she do this teaching thing. She had definitely dug herself one mighty deep hole. On the other hand though, Monica's moves underscored just how inexperienced Jack was at handling female flirting. The impersonations she did in his office had been intended as humorous, but nothing about how he kissed had been a laughing matter. The kisses started as innocent, but when they escalated on both sides until they were deep and rich, she froze and pulled away, remembering she wanted to give him the chance to play the field for a while before staking her claim.

To save them both, she had pretended the kisses were only for the sake of the lesson, but that was a sham. She liked kissing him—really liked kissing him.

She liked it enough to want to be the only woman to ever kiss him again. Deep in her heart, she knew he deserved to experience the full spectrum of the dating game, and all the attention he had missed. He had to know, really *know,* that he was a man worthy of the chase for who he was, not just how he looked. Anything less would not help his confidence. But getting Jack to realize how wonderful he was, and also make him believe it by releasing him to women on the prowl to confirm, was a big risk.

Take it slow. Let him experience everything he never had. She winced. The thought of Jack being with anyone else clawed at her heart. Long before he turned into Brad Pitt, Jack was special. He was a good man, a really good man. Strong, principled, and a hard worker. A man worth the effort she was about to put into him and helping him realize just that. If the dimwit couldn't see what a great catch he actually was, then she'd have to nudge him toward the revelation. She was just the person to help him figure out which women were just there for his new good looks, and which women, rather which *woman*, would make him see he had always been a desirable man, instead of a darn fool nerd.

She stopped in front of the full length mirror. Much better. She looked good. The doorbell rang, and she heard the door open.

"Anyone home here? I'm hungry." The door banged closed, and Jack's footsteps echoed across the wooden floor before stopping at the bottom of the stairs. "You up there?"

"Coming," she shouted back. She sprayed on her favorite perfume, brushed a light blush onto her cheeks, and dabbed on lipstick. She sprang down the steps, her best smile on her face until she saw him.

Suddenly, her plan felt wrong. He looked great. How could she possibly think he needed any pointers? He was handsome now and oozed sex appeal. All he needed was to smile, and the ladies would do the rest. *And that was exactly why he did need her*. She walked down the steps, noticing the white shirt he wore perfectly showed off his broad shoulders in elegant contrast to his tanned skin. His smile shouted confidence even though she knew he probably felt quite the opposite. The way he looked, letting him out alone would be like putting blood in the water to attract all the female sharks out there.

Mentally, she took a calming breath. She'd already been trying to cap the volcano building nerves inside at the thought of helping Jack sort out the bad girls from the good girls, and then giving him the go-ahead to flirt with some pageant-princess—just so she could critique his emerging man-style. But she would have to. Noble as Jack was, if she led him out like a lamb to slaughter, someone like Office Monica might just flirt her way to becoming his first wife. No way would she let something like that happen. She would have to spend the evening with Jack and pull this schooling off, making sure he had a great time learning.

If she could actually bring herself to go through with tonight's lesson.

She chased the anxiety from her stomach and pursed her lips. Not to kiss Jack, but to let out her version of a wolf whistle. "Wow, you look great. This geek-to-chic thing is making my heart skip a few beats."

Arms extended, he turned in a circle. "Have I

impressed you a little?"

Kinley tossed her head. "More than a little." She circled him, smoothing out a shirt wrinkle at his shoulder as she did. "But I did pick out this shirt and those pants, so I knew they'd look good."

He took her hand in his when she touched his cheek. "And look at you. You look pretty good yourself."

She knew the tunic clung to her curves in all the right places and danced around her hips when she moved. "Thanks. This top blew my budget for the week. I couldn't afford to get anything to wear underneath it."

Jack nearly chocked. "What did you say?"

Kinley grinned and grabbed her shawl from the chair. "I'm just trying out some bad girl lines." She stopped by the table near the front door and retrieved a small notebook from the drawer. "Here." She tossed the pad in his direction so he could easily catch it. "Write this down word for word—avoid women who tell you they are not wearing underwear."

He flipped through the empty notebook. "Plenty of room for phone numbers in here."

"Ha. Ha," she said with a flourish. "Don't get overconfident. You still are a dating novice underneath that great face. Tonight is for learning, not practicing, *comprende*?"

"Yes, Miss Adams," Jack replied in his best schoolboy sing-song voice.

Kinley shook her head, "I can see we'll have a bang-up time tonight."

****

Outside, the stars sparkled overhead like diamonds.

The air was crisp, not too cold, but just enough to give Kinley an excuse to slide her arm around Jack's waist and snuggle close.

Jack ushered her into his car. "Are you cold, or are you teaching?"

"Both. What should you have done when a woman puts some moves on you like this?" She slid into the passenger seat.

"That would totally depend on the woman and the moves." He closed the door before she could respond. When he opened the driver's door and got in, he was still talking. "And if I was at all attracted to the woman in question. Want to hear my take?"

"By all means. Say the woman was the Office Hussy Monica. What would you do?"

He started the car and got the heater adjusted before talking again. "Office Hussy?"

"I had another word for her, but I'm a lady." She fluttered her eyelashes.

He laughed. "Actually, that's a pretty good description." He backed the car out of the driveway and started down the street. "Let me set the scene. Monica called me because she crashed her hard drive. I, being the gentleman I am, rushed to her side to help her."

Kinley rolled her eyes. "Oh, geeze."

He narrowed his eyes. "Hush. This is my scenario." He cleared his throat. "As I was saying, I rushed to her office, and put my magic fingers to work."

"On the computer keyboard only."

He laughed louder. "Get your mind out of the gutter. She became very grateful after I recovered her files."

She cocked her head. "How grateful?"

"*Extremely* grateful."

"I'm sure."

"I got out the trouble report for her signature, and she took it, making sure her fingers tangled with mine."

"Good Lord." Kinley crossed her arms and sighed.

"Then…" he dragged out the word to silence her, "She walked to her desk and leaned *way* over, pretending to get a pen from the top drawer when a perfectly good pen lay on the desktop. I could not help but notice how her skirt rode high up her thighs." He winked. "She made no attempt to adjust it when she turned to face me."

Kinley's head jerked. "You looked away, right?'

"Not exactly. She rested her backside on the desk, and motioned me over. I suddenly felt stockinged toes climbing up my pants leg as she was signing the work order."

Her eyes widened.

Had he encouraged her?

"So you went from fixing a computer to playing footsie with a skank in an isolated office?"

His smile grew. "If you let me finish, I'll tell you what happens next."

"Well, you certainly have my attention." She tossed her hand. "By all means, continue."

"I moved away, but she slipped on her stilettos again and followed me."

"She had taken off both her shoes?"

"She did."

"Why?'

"Not sure. I would have asked her, but she suddenly asked if you and I are a couple."

An eyebrow inched upward. "What did you tell

her?"

He hushed her with a finger to his lips. "My story. I'll talk, you listen. I didn't get a chance to answer before she began telling me exactly how she liked guys to kiss her and"—he raised his eyebrows up and down like Groucho Marx—"and do more stuff. She asked me how you liked to be kissed, then she suggested all sorts of inventive things, playing like she was counseling me on what women like."

Kinley felt the heat of a blush move across her face. Was he teaching her a lesson? "Jack, what are you doing?"

"Taking your pop quiz, Teach."

"I think you are enjoying the lesson a bit too much." She shook her head. "But, if I had to grade you right now, you'd get an F."

He laughed. "The real answer is, I would move away and leave the room. I was just going for extra credit." His expression turned from playful to serious. "Want to hear what I would do if the woman was someone like you?"

The heat in her cheeks ramped up a notch, and Kinley was grateful the cool night air would hide it. "Jack…" She stammered. "You don't know what you'd do. Every situation is different."

"That's what makes the whole shebang seem upside-down. Suddenly everything's changed, and just because I look different. All the years Monica and I worked together, when I passed her in the hallway, she never would even look at me. No women really did. But now I must have met every woman in the place, and maybe a few from the office building across the street, too. All this attention feels weird. So weird, I'm considering becoming a recluse. Unless you can turn back time to before the accident so we can have the Chinese delivered, and things return to normal."

Kinley nodded. "I can only imagine how awkward it must be for you."

Jack glanced at her, and then back to the road. "Not sure how to take that. Awkward because I'm a bumbling idiot around women, or awkward because I'm older and should be wiser?"

She looked at him, wondering if she was helping or hurting, and then quickly looked away. "Neither."

"Kinley, I appreciate your help. I really do. But sometimes I feel like I'm Frankenstein—the old guy, not the hot new one—and the ladies are part of a mob with lighted torches coming to get me."

"Aaron Eckhart is pretty hot." Kinley smiled and angled her head. "You may look a bit like him." She touched his cheek. "And you do have some pretty sexy scars."

Jack shrugged away her hand. "You, too?"

Kinley's mouth fell open. She hadn't expected something like that. "No."

He looked at her until a car horn made him focus on the road. "Sorry, Kin. I'm processing a lot of stuff. I'm a grown man and I can take care of myself to an extent at least, but what I really need from you is advice, not product testing."

Kinley bit her lip. Unconsciously she'd been lecturing him like a drill sergeant, probably making him feel worse than he ever had about women and dating. For a while, she'd back off and let him find his way. Even if it meant she'd have to stand by and watch every woman in town flirt with him. "You're right. No more product testing. I'll hang around for moral support." She smiled. "I know you'll do great." When she saw Jack smile back, she felt her heart cartwheel.

I can do this. She could toss him into a dating pool full of female sharks, without a life preserver, and watch what happened. Many times she'd heard the longing in Jack's voice when he talked about watching guys get the attention while he sat on the sidelines like a second-string player. The accident had given him a chance to finally get into the game, and she couldn't take that away.

But being a cheerleader on the sidelines wasn't exactly what she had in mind.

Chapter Eleven

A few minutes later, they were sitting at a table in Verve, a small trendy restaurant in an even trendier part of town. The place was packed, both at the bar where patrons waited for a table, and in front where those without reservations waited for a cancellation or no-shows. On the way to their table, Kinley could have sworn it was no accident when two women bumped into Jack, the redhead dropping her purse at his feet. Their polite 'excuse me's' were laced with a little too much animation, not to mention the roving gazes of appreciation that ran down Jack's form.

The Purse-dropper bent down to retrieve her bag at the same time Jack did, making sure her low-cut top dipped even lower.

Jack could not help but look right at what she wanted him to see. He fumbled for the bag, picking it up and dropping it twice more, before he finally straightened and handed it to her.

Purse-dropper glanced at Kinley before planting a kiss on Jack's cheek and whispering a much too sultry 'thanks'.

Once seated, Kinley practically tore the menu from the waitress' hand. "Can you believe that?" She huffed. "So blatantly obvious."

Jack looked around the room. "What?"

The perplexed look on Jack's face showed she still

Kathye Quick

had some work to do. "You know that woman dropped her purse on purpose."

"Why would she do that?"

Kinley sighed loudly. "So you would pick it up, of course." She lowered the menu and leaned forward. "You have to start paying more attention to the signals."

Jack laughed. "You sound jealous."

"That's unfortunate because I intended to sound mad."

"At me?

"Yes. No. Maybe." She wrinkled her nose. "Look at you." She put down the menu on the table and jerked her hand in his direction. "You could ramp up the heartbeat of a nun. I guess until you figure out how to maneuver in the dating minefield, I will have to go out in front and defuse the bombs before you step on them and blow up yourself." She shifted in the seat, settled, and then shifted again. "You probably didn't notice, but a few heads turned when you walked in."

"You're right. I didn't notice." He glanced around the room.

Three women waved.

Kinley rolled her eyes when he waved back. "Stop that! You're encouraging them."

Jack laughed and then reined in his smile when Kinley didn't respond. "Has anyone ever told you how cute you look when you're mad or jealous or whatever you are at this moment?"

"Mad," she volunteered. "I hate when women look at you like you're lunch, and they haven't eaten in days. I want to smack the drool from their faces."

Jack turned a page in the menu. "Now *that* I'd like

130

to see."

Kinley shook her head. "If you can't be serious right now, just figure out what you want and order."

Jack perused the choices, and Kinley watched him over the top of her menu. She should really apologize for her snippy attitude. None of this was his fault. He went out for Chinese and came back with a new life, a really foreign life. All week long, she had been looking at the situation from different angles, and came up with the same conclusion. Jack's new face wasn't the problem—Jack was.

He was absolutely determined to ignore the changes the plastic surgeon made, and assume this attention thing was just a phase—that the women would go back to ignoring him once they realized he was just as boring now as he had been before the accident. The assumption was downright crazy.

Jack was never boring. He just never let anyone get too close. Before the surgery, he made choices that allowed him to blend into the background. The extra weight and the sloppy clothes told everyone he wanted to be left alone. But nothing would ever be the same for him, and she had to shoulder part of the blame. The new clothes, the contacts, the haircut were all her idea. She would have to find a way to handle the consequences of turning him from the frog he thought he was into the prince she *knew* he was.

The tapping of high heels crossing the wooden floor and heading right for their table made Kinley sigh. She concentrated on her menu. *Keep going, keep going.* But the footsteps stopped, forcing her to face the women who owned the shoes. The purse-dropper.

"I just wanted to thank you, again. I mean, who

knows where my bag would have ended up if you didn't rescue it," she said.

Purse-dropper's voice sounded like a purr. Kinley sighed and swiveled in the chair. *Here we go.* She propped an elbow on the table and rested her chin on her knuckles. She hoped the frozen smile on her face would send the interloper a distinct message.

"Anyone would have done the same," Jack replied with a dismissive wave.

The woman put her hand on the table and leaned forward. "I'm glad *you* did.'

Kinley rolled her eyes and signaled to a passing waiter. "Cosmo and step on it." She grabbed her water glass and chugged down most of the contents to keep from talking. She'd see how Jack handled this.

Jack stood. "Glad to help."

Kinley saw his expression change, and a pleading look settled into his eyes.

Purse-dropper's smile suddenly faded. She finally looked at Kinley. "Are you with her?"

The waiter brought Kinley her drink. As she accepted it, she pasted on a smile, and made sure she kept eye contact with the women. *Hey genius. I've been sitting right here all along. Stupid questions deserve brilliant answers.* "Not only am I with him, but today is our anniversary. We've been married for ten years. Want to see the kids?"

The woman plastered a hand over her cleavage and sprang upright. "I'm...no."

"Have a nice dinner," Kinley called as Purse-dropper finally left. She turned to Jack. "And that's how you handle a woman like her."

"Well, that was awkward," Jack said.

"For her. For you, better get used to women like her circling like vultures."

He shook his head. "Amazing, all this attention from my face slamming against thick glass is unbelievable. Maybe I should have done something like that years ago." He laughed.

As an image of Jack thrown against the windshield flashed through her mind, she felt suddenly cold. She didn't return the laughter.

Jack knew his attempt at humor had fallen flat. "Sorry, I meant it as a joke."

"Not funny at all, Jack." She guzzled the rest of her drink.

Jack reached over and took the glass from her hand. "Something is definitely bugging you tonight. Want to tell me?"

She didn't answer him immediately because over his shoulder she could see a woman staring at his back. The woman smiled when she saw Kinley, a smile that Kinley recognized as a subtle challenge. Jack might not notice, but women knew these things. The first chance that woman had, she would be coming for Jack.

"This place is normally okay, but tonight the noise level is out of control with more than the usual amount of estrogen in the air. Would you mind terribly if we left?" she asked him. The way Jack leapt to his feet told her that he didn't mind at all.

He pulled out her chair. "We'll get takeout for dinner."

"I don't think so," she replied as they headed for the door. "Last time didn't go so well. We'll order from a place that delivers."

****

133

"Never thought I would appreciate the taste of fried onions on a burger as opposed to filet mignon." Jack bit into the dinner delivered from the corner deli. "But since I left the hospital, even the simple things are better."

"You've been through quite an ordeal. I thought I lost you for a while there." She shook off the feeling of dread that always came when she thought back on that day. She tried to concentrate on the present, but as she did, all she could think about was how much she enjoyed being with Jack. The feelings she had kept growing each time they were together, and she felt another surge of delight, like champagne bubbles sparkling, just from watching him tear into his burger.

"What are you thinking?" he asked when he saw her smile.

She couldn't tell him the truth, not yet. "I'm just hoping you aren't getting too tired with being out this late after working all day. I know that slave driver boss of yours is probably pushing you, and I don't want you to get sick or relapse."

"Rashesh isn't a slave drive, Kin." Jack ran his palm across the back of his neck. "He doesn't make me do anything. I like to work."

"How well I know."

"Thanks for worrying about me, but I couldn't feel better."

Or look better. "You're still recovering from a lot of broken stuff, not to mention more than a few surgeries on that mug of yours. No way you're even close to a hundred percent. You should be working only part-time, but I'm sure you get there by six a.m. and stay well past dark most days."

"Wow, didn't think you noticed. Maybe being in that accident wasn't such a bad thing after all."

"Hey, don't say things like that. If you give me a bunch of grief, I just may stop caring about you." She didn't mean that. Thinking about him smashing into his car windshield just triggered a fear reaction.

"Sorry, Kin. Beyond sorry. I'll never tease you about that again as long as I…"

Kinley could feel her heartbeat begin to rise. *I can't let him finish that sentence. I can't let him say any more.* She stopped him the only way she could think of at the moment. She leaned over and kissed him,

About the same time her lips touched his, she realized her impulse may have been a mistake. Jack didn't pull back and totally reject her, but his eyes opened wide.

He dropped his burger and his shoulders locked.

Quickly, Kinley rocked back and closed her eyes, conjuring up a pool of quicksand to sink into. Her mind raced with a hundred ways to apologize. Maybe he'd believe she had gotten gas from the take-out, and it made her lurch forward. Or maybe she could convince him she felt a slight earthquake, and it made her jumpy. Not knowing what she would find, she slowly opened one eye. Jack was smiling, so she opened the other.

He reached out and traced the curve of her cheek right before his fingers sieved though her hair. He cupped her head gently and pulled her toward him.

She looked at his lips, and watched them come toward her, honing on her mouth as sure as a flower seeks sunlight. She dropped the soda can she still held, not caring the contents were now on her new rug.

Then he kissed her, and instantly the connection

fused her to him. They had kissed before, but it had never felt like this. Emotion poured out of Jack like he'd been holding back for a few decades. Kinley had felt the sparks in their kisses before, but this time, Jack's kiss felt more like what she imagined happened when flint strikes steel just before the kindling bursts into flame.

She heard him groan as if the sound had been trapped inside him.

Gently, he took her elbow and urged her to standing. Utensils rattled off the coffee table they brushed against as they rose. He took a step closer, his mouth tasting her, kissing her then his arms swept around her, caressing.

His kiss held such gentleness that it made her head spin. Kinley could feel herself responding in the most elemental way. She reacted to his heat, his heartbeat, his enjoyment—her heartbeat rising.

His kiss deepened, and her lips parted against the pressure. Tongues first touched and then tangled, and suddenly, she couldn't catch her breath or her common sense. Good judgment skirted her mind, trying to slip in between the kisses. Each time she started to listen, Jack's tongue would swirl against hers, and she chose to pay attention to his kiss and to experience the sensations the contact brought instead of the sensibility that tried to break into the moment.

All she wanted was to experience everything that was Jack. His emerging beard caressed her skin with delightful scrapes. His breathing, laced with the music of desire, roared in her ears. Everywhere his body touched hers, her skin exploded with heat she imagined could fuse rock.

Then slowly another emotion rose inside her. Uneasiness first whispered and then screamed so loud she had to acknowledge the call. She knew what desire felt like, and knew the onus that often came with following where the emotion led…but did Jack? From what he told her many times, he never got to fully explore the possibilities relationships brought before his dates would shut him down. What would he do when offered the chance to go farther?

"Kinley."

She heard Jack's rough murmur, and thought he might stop kissing her, but his mouth came right back down on hers after he said her name.

"Kinley."

He whispered her name again, his warm breath moving across her lips, sweeping her fear and common sense away. She could do no more than kiss him back with every ounce of excitement he released inside her. All this time she never dreamed Jack might want her. All this time she hadn't really admitted to herself how much she wanted him. All this time. All this wasted time.

"Kinley." This time, he lifted his mouth. His fingers brushed her hair and then her forehead.

She saw his gaze drop briefly to her lips before returning to her eyes. "I lost my head," she heard him say. She wanted to tell him she didn't agree, but couldn't seem to think straight with the wild sizzle that ran through her veins and short circuited her mind. So what if he lost his mind, and she lost hers. Would that be so bad? She was about to tell him that when she saw a frown crease his forehead. His gaze cut away from her face, and she heard him take a deep breath.

"I should probably go." He headed to the door.

She knew she should say something, but her heart still pounded and her mind still whirled with questions. Try as she might, she couldn't form the words.

At the door, he stopped. "I know you didn't mean for that to happen, so let's just forget it did, okay?" He stepped out and kept on going. "I'll see you tomorrow," his fading voice called back.

A helpless feeling rose to a crescendo when she got to the door in time to see him stride to his car. What had just happened? Her heart still pounded, and the rich rush of desire hadn't faded, but Jack was gone. She speared the front curtains with her hand and looked out. Jack's car was still in the driveway. What must he think about her? Had she turned into the very kind of woman she tried to warn him against?

He loved her. He had to love her. She'd finally come to realize their friendship was moving in that direction for a while, and until Jack's accident, she truly thought she had time to be sure. But the hard lesson she learned about how quickly someone could be taken away changed everything.

She wanted to give him the time he needed to find his way around this new life he'd been handed before springing the *I think I love you* scenario on him. But what the surgeons did to his face, albeit a perfect masterpiece, made her rethink her perfect plan. Maybe trying to help him notice women, and handle the attention from them because of a face that now looked like a Greek god, wasn't such a great idea after all.

Where was a time machine when you need one? If only they could go back before the accident, before things got so complicated. She snickered. Then what?

The accident was the catalyst that made her finally admit how much she did want Jack to be a permanent part of her life, and bring along his bits, bytes, and supercomputer brain.

Think, girl. Time to go to plan B.

But unfortunately, she never had a plan B. Somehow she had to find a way to show Jack that moving from the love of a friend to something more was not the end of the world. She knew Jack had feelings for her, serious deep feelings. He couldn't kiss her the way he had if he didn't. There had been no friendship in those kisses. There had been so much more. So if Jack did feel the same way about her as she did about him, what was the problem?

Was there something she didn't know? Was there a reason Jack could not or would not love her?

****

Jack sat in the car staring at Kinley's front door. The opportunity to let Kinley know how he felt had just been handed to him on a silver platter. Why had he hesitated? He grabbed the steering wheel with both hands and bounced his head back against the seat's headrest.

Guilt could be the only answer. He wasn't the man Kinley thought she'd known for the past two years. Though the accident had changed his face, nothing could change the fact he had been lying all that time.

He couldn't deny something was definitely different between them. The way she looked at him, the overheated kisses, all played havoc with his senses. He suspected she wanted him to think the student-teacher role playing was for his own good, something any friend would do to help, but too much had been happening between them for him to actually believe that was true.

In a perfect world, this story would have a happy ending. They'd start out on a perfect date and end up admitting their feelings for each other, and then live happily ever after. But there was one glitch in that fairy tale—the prince never lied to the princess. Maybe he looked like a prince on the outside, but inside, he was still the frog.

In wanting to keep Kinley interested, he had been content to let her think he was the consummate geek, someone she could trust, someone who would not try to hustle her with hollow compliments and the typical moves of a player. The ruse all seemed so innocent, and he had been meant to play the role for only a little while, but a week turned into two, and then a month turned into a year. Before he realized what happened, two years had passed. Now he felt no different than the guy who handed women a line to see what was underneath their blouses.

He was a smart man. He had built an empire by writing computer games. So why couldn't he hack into the supercomputer that was Kinley, and write a code that would clean up the mess he made? The answer was easy—computers were logical and emotionless, and easier to repair than a broken heart. If he handled his confession wrong, not only would he utterly disappoint Kinley, but he would probably lose her forever.

Chapter Twelve

The next day, Rashesh came into Jack's office, paging through three inches of reports. "You didn't hear one thing the CFO said during the whole two hour meeting." He stopped flipping through the pages and pointed. "You have some decisions to make right after you sign this."

"What is it I'm signing?" Jack reached for a pen.

"My point exactly. I could be getting you to sign over the company, and you'd never know it until I removed your name off the door." Rashesh hitched his thumb over his shoulder. "By the way, who took your name off the door?"

Jack opened his top desk drawer and retrieved the brass nameplate. He held it up. "I did. I was afraid Kinley might see it."

"It's a little too late to worry about that. Gaming's Prospectus has been made available, and the underwriters are assessing the market value of shares. The firm predicts a huge interest in the stock once this company goes public."

"I still am not sure I made the right decision to go public," Jack replied with a shake of his head.

"Don't doubt your gut, Jack. You always make the right decision in business matters when you listen to that voice down deep inside you. The investors will make a ton once the IPO is released, giving you enough accessible investment capital to leverage the predicted growth potential, build a new business campus, and hire enough staff to handle it."

"The numbers look good on paper. I only hope all goes according to plan, and no one loses money on the deal."

"Let the underwriters worry about that. You stay focused on the company and making sure it seems solid and successful during the quiet period before the IPO is officially offered. That way, the potential trading price will be high when the market opens to the public. Unfortunately, though, once the stock hits Wall Street and the media jumps on this story, your face will be in the papers and on the news whether you like it or not. I'm busting my butt at keeping the lions at bay now. Just wait a week. I won't be able to hold them off at all." He grabbed a pen from among those on Jack's desk. "Here. Sign."

Jack scribbled his name on the line marked with a tab. "One thing at a time. What did I just sign?"

Rashesh was about to answer when the door to the office opened.

Kinley's brother walked in. "Hey, Mr. Patel, I found the glitch in Mega Wars."

Jack and Rashesh looked up in unison.

When Mike saw Jack seated at the desk, Mike's brow furrowed. "Hey, Jack, what are you doing here, and why are you in a suit?" He walked to the desk, his gaze scanning the top. "Did you get a promotion or something?"

Jack bolted to his feet. "Kind of."

"Cool." Mike turned his attention to Rashesh. "You know that part in the game when you match a whole row of weapons, but instead of giving you more ammo, the game blanked out?"

Rashesh nodded.

"Fixed it."

Jack could hear the pride in Mike's voice. He had been just like Mike at that age—into video games and computers, wide-eyed and innocent of a sort, with one big difference. Mike had no problem with the ladies. Things certainly had changed. Nowadays, girls appreciated brains as well as brawn. He shrugged. He had been born about fifteen years too soon. Wait. No, he wasn't. Then he wouldn't have met Kinley. *Never mind*. He was good with things as they were. Sort of anyway.

"When did we…" Jack feigned a cough to cover the slip. "Rashesh hired you?"

Mike shrugged. "A few days ago."

Jack glared at Rashesh. "I didn't know."

"Mike is really good with finding glitches in the system. I couldn't let the competition get him."

"They wouldn't have. He leaves for college in a few weeks," Jack said.

"Still, he did fix Mega Wars," Rashesh reminded him.

"I would have gotten to that," Jack waved a hand in the air.

"So you did get a promotion," Mike piped in, looking at Jack from head to toe. "No one in Troubleshooting wears a suit. If you want to still fit in with the Nerd Herd, you better go back to jeans and a T-shirt."

"Jack's more Research and Development now," Rashesh offered.

Mike shrugged. "Oh. Also cool."

Rashesh motioned to the door. "Why don't you get down to programming and let them know how to get around that problem."

"Sure," Mike stopped at the office door and looked back at Jack. "Does my sister know you won't be driving around all day in the Nerdmobile anymore? I know that will make her really happy. Since the"—he smacked his hands together—"you know, she worries about you."

Jack willed his guilt to settle. "I was planning on surprising her."

"Nice." Mike nodded. "Maybe she won't be so crabby then." With a laugh, he walked out.

Jack did a slow turn to face his partner. "You hired him." He punctuated each word with a pause for emphasis.

"The kid's brilliant."

"I know. How long do you think before he figures out I'm not who he thinks I am? Then, how long after that do you think before he tells Kinley?"

Rashesh didn't make eye contact. "One question at a time," he replied before falling into silence.

"I'm waiting."

"I'm thinking."

Jack dropped his shoulders. "This mess is not your fault."

The tension on Rashesh's face lifted.

"Not all of it anyway," Jack continued. "You did hire Mike, so for that you probably should take some of the blame. But the rest is all mine. The inferno I'll have to face for continuing to let Kinley think I'm a techie, instead of knowing I'm the CEO of Gaming

International, is something I have to do alone."

"Darn, I thought I was off the hook for a minute."

"Not by a long shot. What you do is stick close to Mike until I can figure out a way out of this mess."

Rashesh blew out a long breath of air. "How long do you think that will take? I have to fend off the media, finish work on the IPO with the underwriters, and try to keep the bloggers from connecting the dots about you for a little while longer. I have a full plate already."

Jack shook his head. "I honestly don't know. The only experience I have in getting out of tough situations has all been in my imagination, and that will not help me very much now."

****

Upstairs in her bedroom, Kinley could not stop thinking about the big chance she was taking. In the past, she had not taken many risks. None that mattered anyway. She aced her job every day, had a great house, great friends, and even a best friend who could fix anything she could screw up on her computer. But gradually, that particular best-friendship had changed, but she hadn't been ready to admit that until she nearly lost that guy. Suddenly, things were more urgent, more necessary. Suddenly, risks were her only choice.

Every night for a week now, she tossed and turned herself to an exhausted sleep, trying to figure out why Jack would kiss her the way he had and then back off. He returned her kisses, her touches as though he were devouring her. The heat burned hotter than Phoenix in August, and she could not deny she wanted more. But each time she started in that direction, she watched him retreat, freezing up faster than water in an arctic blast.

Why? She had no explanation except one. Jack wanted to explore this new phase of his life. See what the other beautiful people, as he always called them, had to offer.

Memories kept festering in her mind. She'd had her fun growing up. Flirting became second nature in high school, moving smoothly into the play of more serious relationships in college and beyond. Dating had never been a problem. Quite the opposite. Guys hit on her regularly, and she became mighty adept at knowing what to do and what not to do when dealing with the ones who thought they were players. She played the field a little herself, had her fun, and could look back without any regrets.

But the memories were her memories, not Jack's. He was starting from square one armed with nothing more than a brand new pretty face and the proverbial empty dance card that women were now more than willing to fill. In high school, girls learned about boy-girl things by trial and error. Flash forward, and Jack wasn't in high school any longer, and the women were more seasoned. She easily saw how he could get distracted by a shapely backside, and just as shapely a front side now that were both suddenly in play.

Before, he knew he could look and not touch, but now, not only was touching allowed, but encouraged by plenty of women on the prowl. The hussies were out there, ready, willing, and more than able to sink their teeth into someone kind, and sweet, and nice. Someone like Jack. She couldn't protect him from all of them.

Slowly over the time since they first met, she got to see without a doubt that he showed her the best in any man. Probably without even knowing it, Jack had taken root in her heart. Their relationship could be like a wonderful fairy tale come true if only she had told him before that fateful day.

But now it may be too late. Jack would never be overlooked again. Maybe he had blended into a crowd before, but now looking at Jack was like looking into the sun—beautiful but potentially lethal. Without a doubt, and without her help, someone would try to seduce him. For two years, they knew each other with never as much as a hint of anything more than a lasting friendship between them. Now women were suddenly offering him everything he never had a chance to sample simply because he looked great. Could she make him believe she wasn't like them, that she was different, maybe better?

No, not yet. First, Jack had to experience the things reserved for the cool guys and play in the deep end of the dating pool. Anything else than letting him find his own way would not be fair to him or to her, or to anything they could have together until he got the thrill of the hunt out of his system. She knew he would tire of the dating hype eventually. Guys always did. Some took longer than others, but sooner or later even the most proficient dabbler wanted the security of a wife, a home, and maybe some kids. The only question would be when would Jack be ready to listen?

She glanced at the alarm clock on the bedside table. Seven o'clock. Jack was probably hunched over a computer keyboard, working on how 'Dakota' would save the world for democracy in the world Jack was building for about the hundredth time. He probably hadn't eaten, and neither had she. Small talk over dinner would be just what she needed. She hoped he felt the same.

If she could get Jack to come over in the next half-hour, he might be up to some serious kissing. The thought made her smile. She did like kissing him. She walked to the full-length mirror on the wall and checked her backside. The new jeans fit pretty well. Maybe Jack would notice. She could only hope. She reached for her cell phone just as it rang. Judy's information appeared on the Call ID.

"Hey, what are you up to right now?" Judy asked. "I thought we could catch a chick-flick or something. Ron's out of town on business."

"I thought I'd stay in tonight. Maybe fire up the Kindle and read some." Kinley walked to the edge of the bed and sat. "Maybe make a bowl of soup or something."

Judy snickered. "Oh my Lord, you're planning to jump Jack."

Startled, Kinley nearly dropped the phone. "Excuse me?"

"Dish, girl. The Kindle gave it away. You don't have one, and if you did, you probably wouldn't use it. When I asked you about tonight, you thought 'electronic device', so you must have been thinking about Jack."

Kinley sighed. "You caught me. You know I sleep around all the time, so why not with him?"

"Yeah, and I'm from Mars," Judy replied then paused. "Well, being the good girl you are, if you're admitting to wanting to do more than discuss the latest smart phone with him, then he means something to you. He better not break your heart because I'll kill him if he does, and after that, Ronnie will. What's the plan?"

"No plan. Jack's working late. I may just ask him

over for leftovers."

"No soup then," Judy said. "Too easily spilled in the heat of passion. Try oysters. Raw for the full aphrodisiac value. They are supposed to be potent little suckers. And some avocado. In ancient times, avocados were truly the forbidden fruit, being considered a powerful stimulant." Judy laughed. "Bet the combination will steam up Jack's glasses."

Kinley did not find her friend's attitude amusing. "You done?"

"I am. You're staying in then?

"I am."

"And not alone."

"Maybe not." Kinley heard the distinct interrupting buzz of an incoming call and angled the phone "That's Jack," she said in response to the second buzz.

"Well, all right then. Have fun."

Kinley switched the call. "Hey," she said to Jack. "I was just thinking about you."

"I need to talk to you, Kinley. Can I come over?"

Kinley felt a rush of dread flood her stomach. He sounded so serious. "Of course. Hungry?"

"No. I just need to see you."

His tone had not lightened. If anything, he sounded more morose. "Light's on, door's open. Come on over."

Chapter Thirteen

By the time Jack pulled up in his car, he saw moonlit shadows lengthen across the driveway.

Kinley opened the front door and waved him inside. "For someone who sounded like he was in a hurry to get here, you sure took long enough."

"I had a lot of things on my mind and needed some time to sort them out," he replied.

"Three hours?"

He hadn't noticed the time. "That long?"

Kinley nodded.

Jack didn't say anything more before heading for the sofa and sitting.

She sat opposite him in a thickly padded armchair. "You're here now, so talk."

Jack didn't know where to begin. Should he just blurt out everything he needed to say, and then do the old duck-and-cover as he waited for the fallout? *No, Kinley deserves more.* She deserved an explanation along with the truth, He took a deep breath and tried to begin, but then he noticed how the light from the lamp glistened off her hair, caught her profile, the soft curve of her cheek, and all he wanted to do was touch her, not talk. For sure he didn't want to bring up issues that would put a deep chasm between them.

He shifted. "Kinley, from the time I noticed my first whisker and realized girls didn't get them, too, I knew my place. I've worn glasses since first grade, and never outgrew the baby fat like my aunts said I would."

"Ok, but that's the past, and everything has changed now," she countered.

"Remember when I first met you, Kin?"

"How could I possibly forget? I was about to launch my laptop into the back yard. Only your iron grip on my arm stopped me from turning it into a pile of parts." A single note of laughter escaped her. "You were like the superhero of computers, swooping in to save it from certain death at the hands of a madwoman. You are one amazing technician."

"And therein is the problem." After he spoke, he saw confusion dart around in her eyes.

"What do you mean?"

Jack heaved out a heavy breath and dropped his shoulders. Exposing all the humiliating feelings he'd so carefully harbored and hid would be hard. "I always knew I'd never be the guy women would look at and say 'hey, I'd like some of that'." He saw her begin to react, and held up a hand to stop her. "No pity-protest. Hear me out. Almost from puberty I knew my place, and that place was on the sidelines. I learned how to act invisible because I was afraid that maybe, just maybe, some girl would notice me, and then what? Be shot down because once she found out what everyone else thought about me, she'd realize if she got too close, she'd be labeled with me?"

"Labeled?"

"A nerd-lover. A geek-freak."

"Not true."

"You wouldn't know. You're beautiful, Kinley, and your looks didn't happen overnight like it did with me. I have no doubt you did all the things you were supposed to do, like go to the prom, date the football captain, and do the necking thing on Lovers' Lane. I didn't. I knew something was wrong with me, and I knew my looks factored into that feeling. Besides being nothing special, I didn't know the first thing about how to talk to a girl except maybe to talk about how to dissect a frog, or how to solve an algebraic equation." His shoulders lifted in a shrug. "I didn't let any girl get close enough to realize it, too."

"You aren't in high school, Jack."

"Nothing's really changed since then. The girls have turned into women and have perfected their skills. I have no skills to even work on." He felt his shoulders stiffen and his jaw tighten. He knew he was doing a terrible job of laying the groundwork for what he had to say, but if he stopped and tried to regroup like he always did, this conversation would go nowhere. *Again*.

"But your life can be different now, Jack."

"No, Kinley. It can't. I'll always be me, no matter how I look."

"You are so wrong." Kinley shook her head. "Sure, you wore loose-fitting, dark clothes, walked in a slump-shouldered way, and worked really hard to make sure people didn't notice you, but that's all behind you now."

He furrowed his brow. "Not by a long shot. That guy who is always in the back of the room, that was me, is me, and will always be me. Truth is, I never will be a swoop in and save the world kind of guy. I am ordinary."

Her brows knitted in a frown. "You're not."

"I'm a nerd. I'll always be a nerd. I like being a

nerd."

"I think I see the real problem, Jack."

When she sighed, it sounded like pure frustration. "I have no problem." He stood. "I understand my place."

She shook her head. "Did you hear what you just said?"

Jack's face contorted and he raised his hands, palms upward in a pleading gesture. "Yes. I heard me try to explain why I have no problem."

"What I heard was you giving up because you don't think you deserve anything more than being the proverbial wing man." She pointed at him. "But you're wrong. Dead wrong. You deserve the same attention single guys get from the available ladies on the prowl."

Was she trying to convince him, or herself? "Because I got a new face?"

"No."

"Because I look better than I ever did?"

"No. Not because when the surgeon took off the mask, he exposed the hunk underneath. Not because you lost all the extra weight when you did the therapy for your knee, and not because you got new clothes that finally fit you."

He didn't quite understand why she sounded so angry. "Then why?"

"Because you're a great guy, you doofus. The ladies will notice that in you now, too, so you better get used to it. You're about to become a hot commodity, Jack."

"So that's all it took?" He smacked his forehead with the palm of his hand. "Why didn't I run my face into a windshield long before this?"

Kinley threw up her hands. "That's it. I give up. Talking to you seems to be one big waste of my time. There apparently is only one way to get through that thick skull of yours. I have to show you."

When he saw Kinley get up from the couch, Jack felt a rush of relief. He didn't know if she was going for the kitchen to get a pot of water to throw on him, or to the back room to get something to club him with—nor did he care. He closed his eyes, grateful he would have a few minutes alone to gather his thoughts.

The conversation had gotten away from him. He hadn't planned on rehashing his past. He had planned on telling her about his company, and the idea appeared to be brilliant as he went over the plan while driving around for three hours. First, come clean about himself and the company, and then tell her how he felt about her, had felt about her for a long time. She had to feel the same way about him. Hormones, both male and female, didn't rage like theirs did unless something made them explode, something like mixing acid and water. That was it—chemistry. They had chemistry. At least, that's what he was counting on.

But once again, doubt began whispering. Could Kinley really be attracted to a plain, brown-wrapper man like him? Do men really find themselves in a position in which they need help with women like Kinley? Did hunks need rescuing as he did now?

"Jack, open your eyes."

Kinley's voice broke into his wildly rambling thoughts. When he opened his eyes, he was hit by her smile with the force of a crashing wave, taking away his breath and making him begin to panic. Not bad panic. Good panic. The panic you feel when you think you may have hit the lottery, but you aren't sure and are afraid to check the numbers in case you made a mistake. You want to believe, but there still is that little nagging that asks 'is this really happening?' Then it did.

Silky lips pressed against his. Soft curves pressed against him, somehow spinning him around and propelling him backward onto the sofa. Slim legs pressed against him, a knee threatening any future children. His hand moved across the soft flesh of the back of her leg, and at that moment, he thanked the god of fashion design for hiking her pencil skirt up her thighs.

She kept on kissing him, and he felt like his every fantasy rolled into one coming true. Only what he felt wasn't a fantasy. Kinley kissed him like he had never been kissed before. He felt dizzy from the sensations spiraling inside him when she tunneled her fingers in his hair. His ears buzzed as blood rushed through his veins drowning out all sound.

Except for the voice of his conscience. *What am I thinking? I have told her nothing. She will hate me if I let this get out of control.*

He knew his conscience was right. "Kinley, this is nice, but…"

"Don't talk," she muttered softly. "I tried talking. You didn't get it."

Her kisses began again. Pouncing kisses packed with determination and intensity.

"Didn't get what?" he asked, his tone breathless.

"You aren't a nerd," she said between kisses. "You never were."

He felt like he was drowning in the deepening pool of excitement her kisses created, and tried to come up for air, but she kept on kissing him. Before he went under for a third time, he attempted one last desperate plea. "I don't think this is a good idea."

"I do."

"I can feel your hands shaking."

"Of course, they're shaking. I haven't felt like this about anyone since my freshman year in college, so I may be out of practice. And if that's true, you are in for a really long night."

"Kinley, you don't know what you are starting here," he managed to get out between kisses.

She took a bite of his ear. "I love it when you lecture me. It gets me excited."

Better if I don't hear that. "I was trying to make you think."

She laughed and kissed his cheek. "You are, and I'm beginning to think you might not like me all that much."

Not like her? Only almost since the first minute he saw her two years ago. Then the like turned into something a lot more serious, and that something more serious, bringing a need that clawed at him from the inside out, trying to break free and lead to the all-consuming, lose your abandon kind of love he imagined every night since the day they met.

Only she couldn't know that. Not yet. Not until he came clean about the man he really was. "I like you," he admitted carefully, "but you have to know something first." He took a deep breath, unwrapped her hands from his neck, and looked away. "I'm a...."

Then suddenly everything stopped at once—the kisses, the touching, his heart.

Kinley jumped up from the couch. "Oh my God. I

am so sorry. I never gave it a thought. How could I have been so insensitive?"

Her wide eyes looked like saucers peering out from over the top of the tented fingers she had over her mouth. "About what?" He heard his voice crack like it had when he went through puberty.

Kinley began to pace. "Here I am acting like Charlotte the Harlot, never giving any thought to your…situation."

Jack drew down his brows and stood. The excitement that had settled in the pit of his stomach was suddenly replaced by total confusion. "You know about my situation?"

"I can connect the dots. You don't have to pretend with me, Jack. We're good enough friends to talk about it." She put her hand on his shoulder. "You're a virgin."

He looked at her, feeling like he had been body-slammed to the mat by a cage fighter. All the air left his lungs, and he couldn't breathe for a moment. "I'm a virgin?" Stunned, his tone sounded more like a confirmation rather than a protest.

"It's okay. There's absolutely nothing to be ashamed about. I find it rather endearing actually."

Jack stared at her, mouth agape. *This cannot be happening.* Was she on the verge of having the birds and the bees talk with him like he was her little brother? He had to stop her. "Kinley, I'm not…"

With a faint smile, she put her forefinger across his lips to stop him. "Shh. Don't talk." She took his hands in hers and looked deep into his eyes. "I know that you are probably not comfortable addressing that particular issue, but with whom better to talk about something this personal than a good friend. Someone with whom you are close is the natural person to help you."

Jack felt his eyes widen so much that he feared they would fall right out of the sockets and hang in front of his face. "You?" he managed to sputter.

Kinley nodded and pointed at her chest. "Me."

Jack felt like all the air left the room. *This cannot be happening. I've stepped out of reality and into some kind of chick flick movie dream. Any* minute *now I'll wake up.* He waited. But nothing changed. *Oh my dear God, this is real.* The evening had crossed over to the weird side, a dark weird side at that. He tried to form coherent words of protest, but couldn't.

A smile dangled on the corner of her lips. "You want to explore your new-found sexuality. I can help."

As taken aback as he was, for some morbid reason, he felt compelled to hear what she had to say. "How?"

"I can give you advice."

"On sex?" He voice took on a horrified, shocked tone.

"On what women like."

Kinley's offer rolled around inside his head, hitting *no thanks* and *yes, please* responses before his brain settled on *she really didn't mean that.* "In addition to schooling me in the ways of a woman in the mood, you intend to school me in what happens when later on we're both in the mood?"

She lifted her shoulders. "Something like that."

He walked away and then came back. "This is getting out of control. I need to leave." He leaned over and kissed her on the cheek. "See you tomorrow."

"Jack, wait…"

He held up a hand to stop her. "Don't talk."

"But…"

"Shh." Shaking his head, he held up both hands. "I gotta go before you have me ordering x-rated pay per view and taking notes."

****

Kinley couldn't move after Jack left. She kept replaying the evening in her mind. Unfortunately, each time it ended the same way.

Of course, Jack was not experienced. They talked about how he spent a lot of time avoiding getting wedgies or being shoved into lockers when he was younger. He had been so successful in settling into that role that blending into the background had become second nature as he moved from teenager to adult. He never talked about women because he probably never had a relationship long enough to make it past first base, let alone hit a home run.

Her misstep tonight was a game changer. Now she had to go back to square one and rethink everything.

Chapter Fourteen

The next day, Jack burst into Rashesh's office like an out-of-control express train. "Stop whatever you're doing. I have a huge problem." For emphasis, he walked to the laptop on Rashesh's desk and slammed it shut.

Rashesh barely got his fingers clear in time. "Kinley didn't take the great revelation very well I'm guessing."

"It was a revelation, all right," Jack replied, pacing.

Rashesh pointed to the chair opposite his desk. "So sit and tell me."

Nervous energy kept Jack on his feet. "I'm a virgin."

Rashesh started to laugh, but stopped when he saw Jack's face tighten. "No, you're not. I distinctly remember the gamer chick you met during the video trade show a year ago. You didn't come back to the suite until the next morning. Don't try to tell me you were writing code all night—unless that's what it's called these days."

Jack stopped pacing. "Ha. Ha. Very funny. And that happened two years ago. Before I met Kinley."

"So we've established you're not a virgin. Probably a little raw in that area, I would guess, but I assume you know the drill."

"You are not helping."

"And you are not explaining."

Jack slid into the chair opposite Rashesh. "I went to see Kinley to tell her about my double life, but my explanation didn't go exactly as I planned."

"So you told her you were a virgin instead?"

"I didn't tell her anything. She started kissing me, and it got really heated. She started talking…"

"Dirty?"

The warning in Jack's eyes made Rashesh make a zipper motion across his lips.

"She started talking about us," Jack continued, "but my conscience began talking louder. I couldn't let things go any farther until I told her the truth. But I pulled away, and she assumed I did because I was a…" He stopped and raised his hands in an I-give-up gesture.

"Oh-h." Rashesh drew out the word. "Bummer."

He raked his hand through his hair. "After that, there was no going back."

"Did you try telling her she was wrong?"

"Right. Good plan. I should have told her about my sexual encounters. All five of them."

Rashesh shrugged. "Four more than I thought."

Jack glared then pointed to the door. "I could fire you, you know."

"But you can't."

"And why not?"

"Two reasons. I run Gaming International until you tell Kinley the truth."

"True, and number two?"

"Your prowess or lack thereof is the least of your worries." Rashesh opened the laptop and spun it to face Jack. "You're out of time. A few people on the Gamers and Lamers are so close to figuring out the whole thing that they are swapping scenarios on the blog."

Jack walked to the desk and read the Blog title—
Jack Reeves 2.0? Skimming the entry, he felt his heart
rate race. He scrolled down a screen and spotted 952
comments on the blog entry. The last commenter
almost had the story perfect, and added a virtual video
tour of what he thought happened.

"You know the video will go viral. Probably
already has," Rashesh warned.

His brows bumped together in a scowl. "When did
this post go up?"

"An hour ago." Rashesh looked at the screen. "The
comments are still coming fast and furious."

"Can you hack into the blog and take it down?"

"That won't stop anything. Gaming's public
offering is three days away, and presales for War Zone
IV are insane. People want to know about the man who
built the empire from two computers in a garage into a
conglomerate with the number one video game in the
universe. There's no way to stop it, Jack. You are about
to become a very public figure, not to mention possibly
overtaking Richard Branson in the net worth category."

The knot in his stomach tightened. "In other words,
I'm screwed."

"Totally, and not in the way you and Kinley were
discussing last night."

****

The call came in over the Bluetooth. "Where are
you, Jack?"

Rashesh sounded angry, and he deserved to be.
Jack was supposed to be helping his partner with the
mess on the internet. Instead, he was driving around,
trying to figure out a solution to the problem he so

masterfully created. "Forty First and Lakehurst Drive," Jack answered.

"Kinley's place."

"Sort of. Across the street, and three houses down."

"I assume there is no point in asking you to come back to the office and sign off on the IPO."

"Use the electronic signature."

"With that attitude you know I could easily steal your entire fortune and run off to an exotic island country with no income tax and no extradition agreement with the U.S."

"If you do, leave me the keys to the Nerdmobile and take some sun block."Jack thought he heard Rashesh say something in Hindi before coming back on the line.

"What are you going to do? You can't hide much longer. The hackers are hacking, the bloggers are blogging, and before long all the dots are connected. Would you rather have someone instant-message Kinley with the news her mild-mannered computer geek is actually a techno-superhero before you get the chance to tell her? I think not."

"Rash, just hold down the fort, and I'll figure something."

"I sincerely hope so. I really don't like all this deception."

Jack felt a cold chill run up his spine. "Believe me, neither do I."

****

Even when he rang Kinley's doorbell, Jack didn't know if he was making the right decision. But what choice did he really have? He had little time, maybe only a few minutes, to make things right. He started talking when he saw the opening door. "Kinley, I'm not a…."

She held up her forefinger to stop him and pointed to the phone at her ear. Still talking, she motioned him inside. "That's awful," she said to the caller. "And she never suspected anything?" She angled her cell phone away from her mouth and whispered, "Girl crisis. Give me a minute."

Jack headed to the living room.

Kinley paced the hallway.

Every now and then, he saw her walk by and could tell by the look on her face the situation was a little more than just a girl crisis. He caught words like 'liar,' 'heartbreaking,' 'devastating'—serious words indeed.

Nearly ten minutes later, she came into the living room. "Sorry, Jack."

"Something wrong?" he asked.

She nodded. "Sally, Judy's admin assistant, just found out her boyfriend has been cheating for about six months with the copy paper girl."

He could see a darkness move into her eyes.

"Why do guys do that?" Kinley asked. "Why can't men just be honest when they want to end a relationship?"

Was he supposed to answer or just nodded sympathetically? Having no experience as either cheater or cheatee, he simply shrugged.

"Of course, you wouldn't know." She settled in next to him on the sofa. "You're so far beyond that sort of thing."

"I am?" He hoped it sounded more like an affirmation rather than a question.

"You would never lie to someone you cared

about."

With Kinley so close, his conscience began a singsong snicker—*liar, liar, pants on fire*—and felt enough heat from the guilt racing through his body to think he might spontaneously combust any minute.

"Most guys should take a page from your playbook, Jack," Kinley continued.

He shook his head. "I don't think they would want to."

"Men can be such jerks at times."

Jack swallowed hard. *I know. You're sitting next to one of the biggest.* The liar-fire he experienced was making him sweat. He frowned. "Kin, we really need to talk."

She raised an eyebrow. "You have been saying that for a few days now. What's wrong?"

He felt as organized as a tornado. "You have the wrong idea about me."

"I don't think so." She shook her head. "Two years we've known each other. I think I've gotten to know you pretty well."

"I'm not the same as when we first met."

She grinned. "No kidding. You turned into the incredible hunk, pardon the twist on Bruce Banner's fate."

"I can relate more to the green, lumbering, mindless guy."

"Gone are those days. You have to get used to being a boy-toy."

"It's more than me just getting my face fixed."

"I know." She sighed. "Crossing that line in the sand must be hard when you've been used to having the sand kicked in your face for years."

"I felt more comfortable being invisible."

"Life may have been easier, but just like in one of those computer games you love so much, one must adapt. Take Dakota in War Zone. He isn't the same on Level Five as he was on Level One, right? At first, he got shot a lot, but then he learned all the techniques and advanced through the levels. It's the same with dating. You start at level one and progress until you win the game."

Despite the tension he felt, Jack had to laugh. "You're kinda sexy when you geek-speak."

She laughed with him. "Hardly."

He saw her eyes brighten.

"But that does bring an idea to mind," she continued. "How about we collaborate and write a program or something like the Rosetta Stone but for dating? We could make a mint."

Was this the opening he needed? *Easy, Reeves, break it to her slowly.* "Ever think about what being rich would be like?" he asked.

"Every time I play the lottery," she admitted.

"Seriously," he continued. "What if I was rich? Think I'd be the same?"

She reached out and touched his cheek. "Rich and hot, a very deadly combination for you these days."

He furrowed his brow. He'd been rich for a few years and, thanks to the accident, now he was considered hot. He didn't want to be either one. All he wanted was to go back and start over. "Why should it matter?"

"It shouldn't," she agreed, "but, in a lot of ways, it does. The ladies will be all over you like white on rice. How long do you think you could hold out and be chivalrous when women begin their mating dance when they find out not only are you gorgeous, but you also are loaded?"

"I can be very virtuous." *Just not at the moment.*

She angled her body and sank deeper into the sofa cushions. "Seriously. Promise me, you won't turn into a player now that you're gorgeous, and break hearts like the guy who two-timed Judy's staffer."

He saw her mouth tighten."I can see the way women look at you now and…"

He cut her off with a quick wave "Don't worry."

She wrinkled her brow. "Are you all right? You look really upset, and there's a vein throbbing in your neck. Is something seriously wrong?"

"It could be," he confirmed.

****

Kinley fixed some quick grilled cheese sandwiches in the kitchen and glanced at Jack. He busied himself with ripping lettuce into small pieces for a salad, but she could tell he was still upset. He'd hardly said a word since they left the living room. She knew he wanted to tell her something, and she sensed both his reluctance and his need to organize his thoughts. That's why she suggested they eat first and talk later.

She thought back to how comfortable the relationship she had with Jack used to be, before the surgeon's scalpel changed his life and hers along with it. They had gotten close, very close, but she only recently admitted to herself her feelings had changed to something much deeper. Jack had always been a good man. Kind. Thoughtful. Principled. He had everything a woman would want in someone with whom to forge a long-term relationship, but Jack couldn't, or wouldn't, see that.

He needed a nudge, and she intended to give him one the day of his accident. Never in a million years did she think the twist of fate going out for Chinese handed her would change her life this much.

Jack now had the opportunity to finally experience all the things he never thought he was worthy of experiencing. Attention. Flirting. The thrill of the chase, and the satisfaction of the capture. Did she have the right to be selfish and take away that chance? Of course, she didn't.

Revealing how she felt about him right now was out of the question. Too many women were telling him a whole lot of things lately, and she did not want to be lumped with any of them. Plus, in all the time they had spent together, she never even hinted she felt anything more than friendship. Admitting her feelings now might guilt him into doing something he may not want or be ready to do. He hadn't tried to make a move on her either, and he did accept her offer to help handle the rush of attention he was getting.

Maybe she should just bide her time until Jack embraced his new reality. At least, she was qualified to help ease him into dating. She'd danced the dance of seduction before and knew how to recognize the signs in other women. Part of her lesson plan would be to make sure Jack felt like the desirable, sexy man she knew he was, the kind of man any woman would want to spend the rest of her life with, and not the nerd he thought he was. Then, once he believed in himself, she would tell him how she felt. Not a minute before. She turned, intent on asking Jack for a plate, but the moment her gaze locked with his, she moved from friend to fan, and she didn't know what to do.

Jack slipped two salad bowls onto the table. "You okay? You look a little funny."

"I know this will sound shallow, but sometimes, I still marvel at the way you look."

"Impressed, are you?"

She nodded. "No doubt you make every woman's heart go pitter-pat these days."

"I still scare myself when I look in the mirror."

With quick moves, she slid the grilled cheese-laden plates on the table next to the salad. "Then you are the only one you do scare. The rest of us are caught up in major appreciation."

He poked at his salad with a fork. "This is a lot harder than I thought."

Kinley nodded. "The man-woman dance is not for sissies."

"Not that."

"Then what?" she asked.

"Talking."

"C'mon, Jack, you don't have to feel awkward. We've talked about everything."

"Not this."

Kinley put aside her dinner and scooted her chair closer, thinking how easily they used to talk. No subject ever seemed taboo, no nerves infected their conversations or their friendship, but she'd come to notice in the last few weeks love had totally screwed up not only their talking, but everything else. Now, his eyes short-circuited her brain, and just sitting next to him made her feel all warm inside. She didn't seem to know what to do about anything lately. The only thing she knew for a fact was she had to do the right thing for

Jack, even if it meant risking everything she wanted. "You know you can talk to me about anything," she said quietly.

"What if there are a couple of anythings?" His lips set in a grim line.

"Then start with the first one and work your way to the last."

"What..." he paused, folding the edge of the napkin. "What if the first something might make you really mad?"

His dark gaze showed the war inside his head. She looked past him and then back into his eyes. "Then maybe you should start with the second and see how that goes."

He leaned toward her and took her hand. "I'm not a virgin."

Idiot. Kinley felt a rush of heat race up her cheeks. She had put Jack in a most embarrassing situation. She could see his shoulders stiffen and his jaw tighten while he waited for her reaction. She couldn't make light of what he said, and she couldn't seem shocked. The space in which she had to operate just got smaller. "You don't have to be embarrassed, Jack."

Her gaze met his and she saw a play of emotion bounce around in the deep brown of his eyes. With him so close, she wanted to cup her hand around the curve of his cheek and not talk at all. She certainly did not want to rehash issues that would make him any more uncomfortable. So she controlled the urge to touch him by reaching up and tugging on her earring.

"No really, I'm not a virgin," he declared.

"Jack, your love life is not anyone's business, least of all mine. What I did was jump to a conclusion and assume something I had no business even thinking about. You know the old saying about the word 'assume'. Only this time I was the only jerk."

He shook his head. "You aren't a jerk, and that's not a problem."

"Don't be so gallant." She looked at him, and then looked away. "And now I need to explain so we can move on from this...issue. I can't imagine what you must have thought." She lowered her gaze. "There I was offering to break you in like a new pair of shoes, like no one on earth ever recognized how wonderful you are." She smacked the palm of her hand on her forehead. "I am not handling this well." She held up her finger. "And don't try to argue the point with me. Guilt is very liberating when properly placed."

"Kin, stop. You shocked me, nothing more."

"You made a special trip over here to clear up things. I think you were more than a little bit shocked."

"The extent of my shock isn't important right now."

"Everything is important. The wrong woman, the right circumstances, and you could get yourself into really deep trouble."

He let out a long breath of air. "This dating thing is a lot harder than I ever expected it to be."

She sighed. "That's exactly why you need my help. You're a great guy, and with what happened, now you're also very sexy and very vulnerable. There are a lot of reasons women would love to get their hooks into you, and most have nothing to do with the plastic surgeon rearranging a few of your facial molecules."

"I have a feeling I'm hearing the reasons whether I want to or not."

She nodded. "You are. What the doctor did was take off your mask, Jack, the mask you wore to hide the fact you are a fantastic guy.'

A confused frown pleated his brow. "That was no mask. That was me. The Mathlete, not the football hero. The wingman, not the player."

"I don't know who hurt you so badly all those years ago, and I really don't care. You need to get this straight right now. You are anything but dull and boring. You are an extraordinary man. You're kind and patient, and take people for who they are, not how they look. Take me, for instance. We started out as strangers, a wild woman about to kill a computer, and a guy saving one because he had a job to do. You were patient and understanding. You talked me down from the ledge and made me laugh."

"I couldn't let you destroy a perfectly good processor," he said with a smile.

"There's more. You have character and heart. I know your neighbors tell you each time you fix their computers without expecting anything in return. And, what's most important to women, you're sensible and mature. Long-term-relationship mature. Let one mate-hunting, black widow smell blood in the water and—WHAM—you're all wrapped up in her web and heading for the lair."

"Don't those spiders eat their mates after..." He waggled his eyebrows.

"It's an analogy but awfully similar."

Heat danced around Kinley's chest. She could feel her blood pumping faster in response to female hormones turning on all over her body. He understood what she said, though. His throat wouldn't be that particular shade of red if he hadn't. "Men who play games are equally on the hunt," she continued. "Women know that, accept it, and play along. But throw a real man into the mix. Watch out." She pointed to him. "You watch out."

"Okay, okay. I hear you. I know I have a lot to learn, but I seriously doubt things have changed much since I stuck my toe in the dating pool a few years ago and nearly drowned. You can't make a silk purse out of a sow's ear, even if the sow in question is wearing a fancy designer suit."

"Lord love a duck, explaining is like trying to get through to a rock." Kinley walked to the sink and tossed her plate into soapy water. She turned and raked a hand through her hair. "You have an MBA from Harvard so you would think a brain would be inside that head of yours, yet you still don't get it."

"I have a brain, but it doesn't seem to be processing very well at the moment."

"Then maybe we shouldn't talk about this anymore."

He shrugged. "Maybe not."

She took two slow steps and gestured for Jack to get up from the chair. He did, and she looped her arms around his waist and got as close as the law of physics would allow. "You stopped me once, but you will not stop me again."

"Kinley…"

"Shh. I am so tired of you trying to talk."

Chapter Fifteen

Something was drastically different this time, and Jack knew it. One minute Kinley was lecturing him, and now all one hundred and twenty pounds of her had wrapped around him like a warm blanket on a cold night. Physical contact was something he had been avoiding until he said everything he needed to say. But this was like nothing he had ever experienced in his life.

Soft lips landed on his, and curvy flesh propelled him backward against the sink. The way she was kissing him made thoughts of entering any confessional leave him, replaced by a-devil-made-me-do-it dream come to life. Only better.

The wonderful fantasy continued as did Kinley's dizzying kisses, and he let himself get lost in each of them. This is what he always wanted. Him. Kinley. Together. Alone.

Except for an ever-present partner in this love triangle. His darn conscience.

"Kinley, do you know what you're doing?" he whispered between her kisses.

"Shut up, Reeves. Talking gets us nowhere."

She kissed him again. This time harder and with a lot more feeling until he could taste the undiluted emotion pouring out of her and into him. He could feel himself getting lost in her taste, her scent, and the curves of her body. He had maybe a few seconds before reaching a no-turning-back point.

"You seem to refuse to get it," she whispered into his ear before her teeth nipped the lobe.

He groaned. "Oh, I'm getting it all right." Before he went under for the last time, he made one last desperate attempt. "This may backfire, Kinley."

She smiled against his mouth. "I love it when you lecture me. That intellectual tone of yours is very sexy."

"I'm not lecturing you. I'm still trying to get you to think about what is happening."

"I am thinking. About everything we can do to each other."

"I may need a flow chart," he murmured. An arm curled around her waist, tugging her closer.

She suddenly stopped kissing him and arched herself backward. "Oh my God, you *are* virgin." She stepped away and began to pace. "It's okay. I got this." She put one hand on her forehead, the other on her hip. "First, we…"

He caught her on the second pass and pulled her into his arms. "I told you. I am not a virgin, but I'm just not…you know, a player either." The tender look on Kinley's face made him smile. "But I've been told this man-woman thing is like riding a bike; you don't forget," he said right before he kissed her.

"Are you a bike from a store on Rodeo Drive or one from a big box store at the mall?" she whispered between kisses.

"You're Rodeo Drive," he answered with a laugh. "I'm the bike pre-assembled and bought at the box store. With training wheels."

"So this is real. You do want me."

Only like forever. Only like a lion clawing its way out of my chest. Only like a life-sustaining need that began the minute we met. "Yes, I do want you."

"Well good. That's out of the way then." She began pulling him toward the stairs.

Jack hesitated. "Where are we going?"

"Upstairs."

He grabbed her by the hips and stopped her. Just because he was in a love-induced coma didn't mean he had completely lost his mind. "Though I want more than anything to go up these stairs, doing so would be a mistake."

"You know this chivalry thing only makes you sexier, don't you? Most guys would just think 'Well all right, now. Let's party.'"

"I'm not most guys."

She stood on the first step of the staircase. "For the next hour, or few minutes or whatever, can't you please be one of those guys who doesn't talk but simply takes?" She grabbed onto his shirt with both hands and pulled him close, concentrating on kissing him again.

He wasn't exactly sure how he found the strength, but he suddenly heard himself say, "No, I can't. Not now, and not with you."

****

Jack's words hit her like a slap to the side of her head. "What did you say?" She felt like a bucket of ice water had just been poured over her.

"Let's go back into the living room," Jack said, already heading there.

She walked in silence next to him, feeling warmth rise on every inch of skin she had, not in the heat of passion, but in the heat of embarrassment. She had broken out her best Type A Brazen Hussy, and Jack said no. Somehow, she had to get her foot out of her mouth—no, both feet out of her mouth—and save what might be left of the evening. Laughing always seemed to ease awkward situations. She'd try some humor because she couldn't think of any other option.

"You're, right," she said before sitting on the sofa. "We do need to think this though. Besides, I really need to get to a gym and work out more before you see me in my all-together." She pinched her side. "I am putting on some weight."

Jack did laugh. "Kinley, you're not fat."

She glanced down. "Do you think my wide hips make my boobs look small?"

He laughed again. "You're perfect just the way you are."

"Then maybe you don't like how I kiss you." She saw his smile widen.

"If you kiss me any better, I'd get electrocuted from the voltage."

"So, I kiss okay then?" She was happy they could still joke together like old times.

"Yes," he confirmed.

"Then why did we stop?"

He took a deep breath and then blew it out slowly. "It's not you, Kinley. It's me."

Kinley sighed. "I never thought I'd hear the break-up line from you." She stood.

Jack grabbed her hand and pulled her back onto the couch. "We can't break up. We aren't a couple."

Kinley looked at him. "You *are* awful at this."

"And I am trying to explain why," he said.

"By all means, enlighten me." She burrowed into

the sofa cushions.

"If we were strangers, this lead-up dance wouldn't matter. If we just met at a club or a party or something, and if we hit it off, after a few drinks, we'd probably skip all the fine points and get right to business. But because we're friends, everything matters so much more when you care about someone." He tucked a lock of hair behind her ear and smiled. "And I care about you. Really care."

She put her hands over her face. "I am so confused," she said through spread fingers over her mouth. "And you're making my hair hurt." She tapped her hands on her thighs. "Tell you what, let's both not talk for the rest of the evening. We'll pick up this insane conversation later."

"But I really need to tell you something, Kin," Jack protested.

"What was it you said to me?" She tapped her forefinger on her chin a few time. "Oh yes, '*not now and not here*'."

"That's not exactly what I said."

"Close enough."

"Guess I should go then."

Kinley shook her head. "No. You aren't going anywhere for a while. My turn for torture." She grabbed the remote from the end table and pointed it on the flat-screen TV mounted on the wall. "Pay-per-view chick flick, and you better watch. There'll be a quiz later."

****

Halfway through the movie, Jack noticed Kinley had fallen asleep. And so had his arm, which was around her shoulders. But he could have cared less about the annoying sensation of pins and needles running up to his neck. He could hold Kinley like this forever. Or until his arm fell off from lack of circulation, whichever came first.

Another man would have run up those hallway steps when offered the chance. But he couldn't. Kinley deserved more before they took that step. She deserved respect, a commitment and the truth. Most of all, the truth. Until the timing was perfect, and he found the courage to risk everything by confessing, he would be content to just hold her, and watch chick flicks every night, if that's what she wanted to do.

Looking down at her in his arms, strands of her hair falling softly across her forehead, the soft rustle of her breath as she slept, he felt no longer the frog but more like the prince. With her, he wasn't the self-doubting guy he saw every day in the mirror despite the surgery. He was a prince on a quest to do nothing more than be with his princess, and make her smile

Suddenly the words were out of his mouth before he could stop them. "I love you, Kinley."

Half hoping she heard him and half hoping she didn't, he waited. But Kinley only sighed, making him wonder if he had only said those important words in his mind.

****

I love you, Kinley.

Kinley didn't know how she managed to keep her eyes closed and not move. She wanted to grab him and kiss him silly, but a deep feeling of caution held her back. Of course, Jack loved her, but there were so many levels to love. She had thrown herself at him, and he threw her back. She had wanted Jack to say those words, and now that he had, she was scared silly.

Which type of love did he feel? How could she know? How could he?

She didn't like calling him sheltered regarding matters of the heart. He hadn't been sheltered. Not really. More like he had been deprived of the opportunity to experience love on any level other than friendship. Like in one of his video games, every time he tried to move to a higher level, he got shot down. Level failed. Game over.

For both their sakes, she had to be sure Jack understood an emotion as powerful as love came with peaks and valleys, and decisions that could have life-changing consequences, both wonderful and dangerous. Until then, she couldn't let him know she heard him say those words.

I love you, Kinley. Words, separately so innocuous, but string them together, and they could move mountains or change the world. Despite wanting to throw her arms around him and tell him she loved him too, she could not let him know how much she had wanted him to say those important words.

Not yet.

Chapter Sixteen

Inside the fuzzy world between sleep and reality, Jack heard Kinley's voice.

"Wake up. It's morning, and your pants are ringing."

He smiled. That Kinley. Pants ringing. What a funster. He could hardly wait to see what else would happen in his daily dream of her. But then a soft warm caress ran across his chest, bringing him a little closer to waking. He heard Kinley's voice again.

"You better get that call. It's 6 a.m. Must be important."

He recognized the ringtone. *Payphone. Maroon 5.* Nothing significant about the song or the group. He just liked the title. It reminded him of days past, and how far he'd come thanks to technology. He tried to get up, but discovered he was pinned from the waist down by something very warm. Funny. Even though he dreamed about Kinley every night, his dreams never felt this real.

He opened one eye and saw a clearly feminine arm across his chest. As his senses converted from slumbering to awareness, he could feel warmth build along the left side of his body and across his abdomen. He lifted his head. Kinley cuddled next to him, her leg across his thigh. He shifted.

Kinley sat up. "Your cell is in your pants pocket,"

she said, straightening and running her fingers through her hair. "I may have a bruise on my side from sleeping on it." She smiled.

Jack thought he heard angels singing. He wasn't dreaming. He had spent the night with Kinley, albeit curled up with her on her oversized sectional in the living room. Still, he felt awesome.

The ringtone stopped.

"You missed your call, but I suspect you know who tried to find you this early." She hid a small yawn behind her fingers.

Jack brushed the hair from her eyes. "It was Rashesh, and you're probably right about the important part."

Kinley didn't move, and he didn't try to make her.

"Sleep well?" she asked him.

"Uh-huh. How about you?"

"Honestly? I'm surprised you slept at all." She leaned over and kissed his cheek. "Considering this couch is ten years old and not very comfortable."

He sat up and settled both arms around her, pulling her closer. "Being here with you in the morning feels like a dream." He felt her snuggle into him. "A really good dream."

Kinley's fingertip ran down his cheek. "I agree." She laid her hand across his stomach.

His muscles contracted in response. He flinched when she skimmed the uneven skin of the keloid scars on his abdomen through the fabric of his shirt.

"Is something wrong?" she asked.

Jack shifted away her hand. "A few places still sting when touched. The doctor told me I can get the scars fixed, but I don't see the need. No one will ever see them."

"May I?" Kinley asked.

"Why?"

"Because I need to," she said softly.

"The scars look pretty ugly," Jack warned.

"Nothing about you is ugly."

He smiled and kissed the top of her head.

Kinley unbuttoned Jack's shirt and gently traced the scars with her fingertips. "Does this hurt?"

He contracted his stomach. "A little."

Kinley moved back. "I'm sorry."

Jack suddenly felt cold. *This is it. This is when she says she made a mistake not sending me home.* Kinley started to speak, and he held his breath.

"I don't like it when you hurt."

He let out the breath and felt the tension begin to leave his body.

"I have a scar, too," she whispered.

Briefly hit with a mix of confusion and surprise, he took a few minutes to react. "Like from an appendectomy?"

"No. Something else. Something worse than a line from a surgeon's scalpel."

"What is it?" He heard the apprehension in his voice and struggled to contain it. "Did something happen?"

She nodded and lay back into the crook of his arm. "I told you that I dated a liar, but it was more than just dating. What I never told you was, I almost married the jerk."

"Oh." Surprised, he couldn't think of anything else to say.

"He ran off with another woman two months

before the wedding."

"Oh," he said again.

Patting his chest, she chuckled. "Very deep of you."

"I don't know what I'm supposed to say."

Her face softened for a moment. "I don't expect you to say anything." Her expression tightened. "How could I have been so blind not to see the signs? I felt inadequate and stupid. Sometimes, I still do."

Jack's arm tightened around her shoulders. "That's silly. Better you found out before you married him rather than after."

She sighed. "I suppose, but it really hurt." Jack started to say something but she stopped him with a finger to his lips. "Let me finish before I lose my nerve. You think I'm this pulled-together person who can handle anything, but the truth is—Mark...his name was Mark—knocked out all my confidence until I met you." She sat up and faced him. "I wanted to tell you about him. I planned to tell you over dinner, but that damned accident changed everything. I never should have let you go for take-out. It's my fault you had to go through all the surgery and all the pain. Can you ever forgive me?"

"Kinley, it was an accident. What happened was because of someone's recklessness, not because you were hungry." He stroked a hand on her arm.

"But if you...died."

The last word sounded like whispered anguish, and he tightened his hold.

"I don't think I could live with myself if something happened to you."

"I'm fine."

"No, you're not," she challenged. "Everything has changed. It's like the accident put you in an alternate universe in one of your video games. You have to relearn how to adapt and fit in because you can never go back to the life you once had."

"Then just like Dakota, I'll adapt." He hoped the admission would assure her.

"There's more." She swallowed hard. "I've thought about this for a long time. I am being so unfair."

A cold chill ran through Jack. In addition to the 'it's not you, it's me' verbiage, 'I'm being unfair' showed up high on the list of acute relationship killing lines. "How so?" he whispered with hoarseness in his tone.

"I think I've been testing you to see if you would hurt me like Mark did."

He saw moistness gather in the corner of her eyes.

"I've been wrong to do that. You would never deceive me like Mark did."

"I'm not Mark, Kin." A sick feeling filled his stomach. *No, I'm worse.* How could he tell her about himself now, with her confessing what she thought was her deepest, darkest secret? If he did try, she would see him just like Mark, a liar, a hideous despicable liar, and probably never forgive him. He didn't know much about women and relationships, but he did know enough to acknowledge females did not forget things like deceit and lies. In trying to be sure his confession was perfectly timed and politically correct, he just may have sealed his fate forever.

A wave of panic gripped him, and he pulled her back to his side until her head rested on his chest so she couldn't see the turmoil he knew she'd see in his eyes.

He wanted to hold her until she felt better. He'd hold her forever if that's what it took. Maybe he was being selfish again. If the previous evening would be the first and last time they would ever be close like this, he needed the time to last for a while longer. Whatever Rashesh wanted would have to wait. Kinley needed him. It didn't matter why she needed him. It only mattered that she did. He felt her relax.

She trailed her fingers down the inside of his elbow. "We're talking too much."

"I should be quiet then, right?" he asked.

She raised her head. "No, you should kiss me now."

Her lips were gentle on his, and he responded in kind. She felt good in his arms, like she should be there. "Comfortable?" he whispered into her ear.

"Very."

Jack felt content to just hold her. He guessed that in a made-for-television movie, this would be the time the main male character broke down and confessed his deception to the woman of his dreams. But in the same movie, confessions would throw the relationship into a downward spiral and then cut to a commercial after the camera zoomed in for a close-up to capture the look of horror and pain on the heroine's face. Though afterward, the guy and the girl managed to get together by the end of the movie, the road to his and Kinley's happily ever after was filled with deep pits.

He didn't want to see the look of horror on Kinley's face when she realized what a liar he had been. He didn't want Kinley to hurt any more than she already was hurting from a past betrayal by adding a new one. He wished the fates would stop tossing him curve balls just when he was ready to confess. Did all men have timing problems like this, or was his hesitation because he was afraid?

He kissed her forehead. "I'd love to stay here all day with you, but I really should find out what Rashesh wanted. I don't have to listen to voicemail to know he probably lost a report or something."

"Cyberspace must have eaten his homework again, huh?" She laughed.

He loved that sound. "Maybe. But I won't know until I call Rash back." He kissed her again because he didn't know if it would be the last time he could.

She pulled out of his arms and stood. "So call him. But be sure to tell him you'll be busy tonight. Here. With me."

****

Jack came out of Kinley's downstairs powder room, shirt open. He tucked his cell phone back into the pocket of his jeans. "Rashesh is in crisis. I have to go." He straightened his shirt with a shrug of his shoulders and started on the buttons.

Kinley watched his bare chest disappear inch by inch with each he button fastened, hating every minute. "He's always in crisis these days."

"He's just doing his job, Kinley. Give him a break."

The tone of Jack's voice made her feel petty. Like a spoiled child. She knew if work called, Jack would leave. He always had. His loyalty and drive were two of the things she loved about him. But not right at this moment. "So?" she whispered.

He sat next to her and looped his arm around her shoulders. "So if I don't get to the office, Rashesh will keep calling until I do."

She fought the small smile that threatened to break out on her face. "Rhetorical question." She bit down on her lip. "I was wondering what you're thinking."

"About?"

"About us."

"Is there an 'us'?" he asked, eyebrow raised.

"Maybe."

"I know we aren't up to that lesson yet, but, if we were, what would come next?"

She started to laugh, even as her heart turned to mush with the horrified look she saw on his face. "There is no dating play book. We just wing it and see what happens."

Jack let his head fall back onto the top of the sofa. "This socializing thing is hard."

"No worries. I'm here to help." She brushed a curl from his forehead. "First thing, we press Rashesh into service." She couldn't stop herself from laughing. "Maybe not the best wingman, but we don't have time to interview."

Rashesh's ringtone began again, and Jack bolted from the couch. "I gotta go. I'll call you later."

Then he was gone.

For the next ten minutes or so, Kinley sat on the sofa going over in her mind everything that had happened. When she was with Jack, her heart swelled like a balloon with hope. But fear and doubt, with stilettos, always managed to stomp the hope into submission.

Jack said he loved her, and she wanted to believe he did. But how could he possibly know for sure when all he had ever gotten from anyone was friendship?

Suddenly, she felt as though she was standing at the edge of a deep precipice, and the next step she took would decide if she lived the rest of her life with Jack or without him.

Either way, whatever she did decide would be a very big step, and a long way to fall if her decision turned out to be the wrong one.

Chapter Seventeen

Jack walked into Rashesh's office, feeling as edgy as a lion on the prowl. "If this doesn't involve the key to world peace, you're fired."

Rashesh looked up from the laptop on which he had been working and held up his hands. "See these?"

"Yeah."

"Know what they've been doing?"

"Besides calling me away from the incredible woman I've been dreaming about for two solid years?"

"These hands have been trying to save your butt." Rashesh flexed his fingers. "And these ten digits have been busy putting out fires to give you time to tell that gorgeous babe you've been lying. Any minute now the media will have your face on anything that beeps, flashes, or is connected to the internet. When that happens, it's over, Jack."

"I was with her all night, Rash. All night. And even though nothing happened, being together was great."

"Being the ever noble knight, I'm sure." He shifted in the chair. "I may have bought you an hour or so but, otherwise, we are out of time."

Jack slid into a chair near the desk. "What happened? I thought I had a few more days."

"You probably don't have a few more minutes." Rashesh angled the laptop screen to Jack. "AOL has the story on its home page, and CNN has sent out breaking news to its subscribers. The vultures are massing, Jack. I wouldn't be surprised if film crews aren't on their way here now."

Jack scrolled through the CNN story. "Who narced?"

"It doesn't matter at this point. Some hacker got his or her teeth into the rumors and wouldn't let go." Rashesh reached over and clicked onto the Gamers and Lamers Blog. "Einstein457 has pieced it together pretty closely, except he didn't come across the Chinese take-out part yet. Even has a before and after picture posted."

Jack stared at the screen, reading his journey of the past few months as though Einstein 457 had been in his back pocket. The accident, the reconstruction, the rehab—they were all dated and documented like a CIA file.

"Damn, he's good. There's even a link to a virtual surgery so you can follow the reconstruction. We need to find and hire him."

"Or hire her," Rashesh corrected. "All sorts of sites on you are popping up." A few mouse clicks and he was on one site amassing potential love interests for the new Jack Reeves, all cataloged by email addresses and description of what they'd do on the first date. "Take a look at what Honey1976 has in mind."

Jack read the first post. "Now that's sick."

"Read Madame D's plans." Rashesh pointed toward the screen. "It involves chains, leather, and some tools from one of those big box stores. *That's* sick."

"Forget Madame D. I need to do something before this gets any bigger."

The muffled sound of a commotion and the piercing whine of police sirens made Jack and Rashesh look up from the computer screen.

Rashesh walked to the window and separated the blinds with two fingers. "Too late, my man." He waved for Jack to join him and pointed. "Looks like you're headline news. We have Channels 2, 4, and 7, Fox, and News 12 outside."

Jack grabbed the phone on the desk. "Security. Jack Reeves here. Lock the front door, and post someone at the front and back entrances. I don't want any part of any media within 500 feet of my office." He walked to the window and peeked out. "I don't get all the fuss. Nothing's really changed but my face."

"Stop kidding yourself, Jack," Rashesh replied. "More than your face has changed. Gaming International is the fastest growing company in the world, thanks to the War Zone games."

"Companies succeed every day. All this attention is nuts."

"GI has made a lot of people rich starting with War Zone I for the start-up investors and continuing with the Initial Purchase Option when the company went public."

"When did that happen?"

"This morning at the opening bell on Wall Street. I knew when you declined to ring the opening bell, you weren't paying much attention, so I went instead," Rashesh commented.

"Companies go public every day."

"But your company has a frog-to-prince story attached, and inquiring minds want to know about the newly minted wealthiest man in the world."

"Want to know what?"

"How it feels to go from junk to hunk."

"More important things are going on in the world."

"Precisely why you are more interesting. Dealing with wars, the economy, natural disasters, and global warming gets pretty stressful. A feel-good story like yours is a refreshing change from doom and gloom."

Jack walked away from the window and slouched in the desk chair. "Think it would play out like this for GI if I was still the frog?"

Rashesh shook his head. "Never. You'd get a few mentions on the late night news, but all this attention?" He gestured out the window. "Now you are Jack 2.0. People want to know, Jack. What happened? Did you engineer the transformation? Every guy who was ever dissed by the head cheerleader in high school, or had the jock give him a wedgie wants to know what it feels like to go from zero to hero. Plus they want you to tell them in all the down-and-dirty details. To the nerds of the world, you're living the dream, and they want to be a part of it." He patted Jack on the shoulder. "You're a real life Dakota right out of the War Zone phenom you created. No, even better. You're a bona fide, hottie-looking idol in the world of gaming." He raised his hands and looked upward. "You're a gaming god. Being with Kinley shouldn't be a problem now."

"I'm not so sure, Rash." Jack frowned. His mind processed a couple hundred justifications for what he had done—none of them ending with Kinley forgiving him. He wanted her more than he wanted to breathe and was crazy in love with her. But ever since he'd been rebooted, things between them hadn't felt the same.

Not that the changes were all bad. He did look

better, but the frog he'd been before the reconstruction stilled lurked just under the surface. Inside, nothing had changed. He lost his heart to Kinley a long time ago. Now he was in real danger of losing her when she found out he had been living a secret life for two years. Would she understand why? After finding out how much some guy had hurt her, he didn't think so.

"A god?" he asked in a dull, lifeless tone. "How long do you think I'll have to stay in gaming Olympus before the attention dies down?"

Rashesh laughed. 'Considering what you've done to give gamers all over the world hope, probably forever."

****

Busy signal. Again. Kinley hung up the phone. She's been trying for over two hours to get in touch with Jack. At this rate, she'd be having lunch alone. She shrugged. She'd just have to go to his office and drag him out. He probably had his head buried in some computer game glitch or was talking some kid through a quick fix over the phone.

She smiled. Thinking of Jack always made her smile. He was such a good guy, always had been. But now, he was also the type of guy that could cause a woman to take notice because of what was on the outside and fall hard from what she found on the inside.

She'd given him some time to splash around the dating pool. Maybe it was time to get him out, dry him off, and finally tell him how she felt before someone got to him first.

****

"Where's Jack?"

Rashesh turned away from the window in time to

see Kinley's brother burst into the office. "See that circle of bodies on the street?"

Mike looked over Rashesh's shoulder. "The ones with the lights and cameras?"

"That's the one. See the man in the center?"

"The guy with the microphones in his face?"

"That's Jack."

Mike watched Jack struggle with the media crunch. "He better wrap up the photo op. My sister couldn't get through to him, so she called me. She's on her way here."

"Did you say anything?"

Mike shook his head. "Not my story to tell." He glanced out the window to the media crush going on in the parking lot. "Looks like the story isn't Jack's anymore, either."

Mike watched Jack push his way through the crowd of reporters and make it to the front door where Gaming International security guards surrounded him before ushering him inside the building.

A few minutes later, Jack walked into the office. "It's nuts out there. I tried to get to my car but couldn't. Even if I managed, I'd never make it out of the parking lot." He stopped when he saw Mike. "Look, I can explain everything."

"You don't have to," Mike said. "Rashesh filled me in." He took a step forward. "I love my sister, and ordinarily, I'd kick your ass for lying to her, but instead, I'll let her deal with you. You've known her for two years; I've known her all my life. Believe me, nothing I can do to you will be anything close to what she will."

"I deserve whatever I get," Jack agreed as he shook

his head. "I've been trying to get out of here and find Kinley. There's a media barricade front and back, and I'm not going anywhere anytime soon." He picked up the phone started to dial out. "Maybe she can get in."

"No need to call her," Mike piped in. "She's on her way here, and she'll be really ticked off once she finds out the truth."

"Maybe she'll let me explain."

"Don't think so." Mike leveled a warning look at Jack. "I hope you like silence. Once she got mad at my Aunt Ellen. Didn't talk to her for months, and Aunt Ellen hadn't been lying for a couple years."

"I'm doomed then, right?" Jack asked, a knot crunched in his stomach.

"Totally," Mike agreed. "Unless you can think of some miracle in the next few seconds."

Mike had barely finished talking before Jack was back on the phone. "All of you. Start dialing. First one to get Kinley on the line gets the next video game named after him."

****

With the crowd, the barriers, and the police presence, Kinley couldn't get near Jack's office building with the car. She had to settle for a parking lot three blocks away. She rifled through her purse looking for her cell phone. It rang just as she found it. She smiled almost on instinct when she heard Jack's ringtone and saw his name flash onto the screen. "Hey, what's going on there?" She got out of her car and started walking toward his office.

"Kinley, where are you?"

"A block away."

"We really have to talk."

He sounded awful. And he hadn't answered her question. A bee sting-sized awareness gnawed. Something was really wrong. "If we were an item, those would be break-up words."

"I'm serious, Kin. We have to talk. Now."

The bee-sting niggle turned into a snake bite ache. "Jack, what's going on?"

"I just need to talk to you."

"Did something happen to the company?" she asked him. "Is that the reason for all the press? If you lost your job, it's okay. You're smart. Something will come up, I'm sure of it."

A long silence fell before he spoke again. "Where are you now?"

"In front of the deli across the street. I can't get any closer to the building."

"Stay there. I'll send out Mike to get you."

She didn't like the sound of his voice. "Why Mike? Why can't you come out?"

"Please. Just there wait for Mike."

"Okay." The line went dead even before she got out the word. She stared at her phone as it disconnected. This was not good. Not good at all. Veteran daters knew the signs, and she had dated enough to be in that category. The foundation had been laid. She could hear it in his voice. The break-up bomb was about to dropped.

She couldn't help but think she'd pushed him, and he was uncomfortable around her now. She had chased him. Under the guise of helping, she started the kisses and maneuvered him into closeness. He said he wanted to talk, but she wouldn't let him. Fear circled her heart, making her feel like she had made the same mistake with Jack that she had made before. She lost her heart to someone who didn't really love her.

A police officer stopped her at the barricade. "Sorry, ma'am. Unless you work or live on the block, I have to ask you to wait here until we can clear the street."

"My brother works at Gaming International," she said. "He's coming out to get me. Can I get in then?"

"We'll see." The officer gestured across the street. "Stand over there, please."

A young woman tapped her on the shoulder. "I heard you say your brother works for Gaming."

Kinley nodded. "He just started there."

"Do you think your brother knows the owner, and can get me in to meet him?"

"Maybe." Kinley watched some local news crews set up remotes. "I'm guessing all this is because of the owner somehow."

"Sure is."

"What happened?"

"You haven't heard?" The girl pulled out her smartphone. "The whole story is amazing. So cool." A few touches on the screen, and she was on the app for the local news station and connected to the live news feed. "Here." She handed the phone to Kinley.

"And we're back," the reporter said. "Rashesh Patel, spokesperson for Gaming International, has promised a formal statement concerning the future of the company will be forthcoming within the hour." Kinley looked up from the screen. Her heart began to pound. The reporter made it sound like the company was indeed in trouble, but the young women who handed her the phone had said whatever happened was 'cool'. She could not process the contradicting statements into something that made sense.

"Keep watching," the girl said, "It's a better story if you hear it from the beginning."

"To recap," the reporter said, "Video game mogul and Gaming International CEO, Jack Reeves, is virtually unrecognizable as the man he was a few months ago, thanks to the skilled hands of plastic surgeons who totally reconstructed his face after a severe automobile accident weeks before the company went public, making it the largest video gaming company in existence. Jack Reeves is now among the richest men in the world. Reeves' secret transformation was exposed by two fans of War Zone who, with the help of fellow enthusiasts on the *Gamers and Lamers* fan blog, pieced together the facts and put out the story on the internet this morning. Now we all want to know why the secrecy?"

Kinley felt like a cold hand gripped her heart. How could she have been so blind? Jack couldn't care about her. If he could hide another life, what else didn't she know? On the phone, the video feed kept running, and like the proverbial train wreck, Kinley could not look away.

"One theory about the cover-up is that Reeves was afraid the investors might view the company as a bad risk with its CEO's health in question, and pass on the company's pre-sale offering, holding back their potential investments in case the price dropped at the opening bell. Another theory is that Reeves remained silent to ensure the company seemed solvent to protect the investment of those who had already pre-purchased stock at the 'Friends and Family' price set before the stock went public this morning. Concerns about Reeves' health potentially could have sent the price of the stock into a free-fall, causing the investors to lose millions of dollars. The Securities and Exchange Commission is investigating the allegations. We'd like to know what you think. Let us know. Use #frogtoprince and text your comments to the number scrolling below."

The reporter's words settled inside her head, and Kinley realized she had almost forgotten to breathe. Jack Reeves, CEO? Impossible. The Jack she knew was only a Trouble Shooter. The reporter said Jack was also rich. Not true. The car he used before the accident had over 200,000 miles of service calls on the engine.

She looked up from the screen. "Wait. The story is all wrong. Rashesh is the CEO, not Jack Reeves. I know Jack. He's just a tech guy."

"How long have you known him?"

"Two years."

The girl just shrugged. "Guess you didn't know him as well as you thought you did."

"Someone has made a big mistake," Kinley protested, still not willing to believe Jack had lied. But when Jack's before and after pictures appeared on the screen, she knew the big mistake was hers.

"Didn't I tell you?" the girl asked, taking back her phone and glancing at the picture. "He was a mess before, but look at him now." She looked up. "Could your brother get me a job?"

Kinley could not grab on to one thought that made sense. She had to get away and sort out what she just discovered about a man she thought she knew. "You can ask him when he gets here." She started walking away.

"Wait!" the girl called out. "How will I know who your brother is?"

Kinley looked back, a knife-sharp feeling of despair shredding her nerves and churning the breakfast in her stomach. She thought about Jack—the Jack she had thought she knew so well, the Jack who apparently had been living a double life, the Jack she just started trusting. She shook her head. "I have no idea."

****

"Where is Mike with Kinley?" Jack peeked out at the street from his office window for about the tenth time.

"Give him some time," Rashesh answered. "He'll be back."

"You don't think he will tell her everything before I can, do you?"

Rashesh shrugged. "Blood is thicker as they say, but I don't think you have to worry much about Mike telling her anything. With all the media on this story, it would be safe to say she already knows."

Jack glared back. "You are a master at stating the obvious." He walked toward to the office door.

Rashesh grabbed onto his arm. "Whoa. Where are you going?"

"Out to find Kinley."

"You'll never get past the sharks out there."

"What can I do?" Jack asked. He forked his fingers through his hair. "I have to get out of here."

"The only way is to give them what they want; the story of how it all happened and where it goes from here."

"Not until I talk to Kinley. She deserves to hear

201

everything from me. Face to Face. Not from some TV anchor or blogger on the internet."

Rashesh nodded. "I'll do my best."

Alone now, Jack peeled off his navy suit jacket and loosened the tie choking him, but he couldn't force himself to move from his spot at the window. He kept scanning the crowd looking, hoping, praying he would see Mike and Kinley weaving through the mass and heading inside the building. No luck. All he saw was a sea of strangers—some of them pointing, some of them talking into mikes, all of them waiting for him.

He ripped off his tie, wadded it up, and threw it across the room. He had no business thinking Kinley would even listen. No business at all. She trusted him, and he used that trust to hide behind. He was hurting her the same way the first liar she trusted had hurt her. His selfish need to keep her close had backfired. She deserved more. The best thing he could do would be to confess, take his punishment like a man, and then let her go so she could find her real prince.

****

In an hour, Rashesh was back. Alone. "She doesn't want to see you, Jack." He held out his hands in a gesture of finality.

Jack blew out a long breath. "I'll give her a few hours then…"

"Ever, Jack," Rashesh interrupted. "She doesn't want to see you ever."

Jack stood silent for a long while. "Now what?"

Rashesh shrugged. "I'm not great at giving advice to the love-lorn, and I don't think there's an app for this."

Behind them the door opened, and a City Parcel

deliveryman walked into the office. "Man, what the heck is going on in here? I took an hour to get inside the place." He slid a large envelope onto the desk and held out his electronic delivery pad. "Sign here."

"Not now," Rashesh said, waving away the device. "Can't you see we are in the middle of a crisis?"

"None of my business," the man said. "I just need a signature so I can get out of the building alive."

A sudden thought pierced Jack's brain, and he grabbed onto it with both hands. "How much trouble did you have getting in here?"

"Not much. No one pays much attention to a package guy in navy shorts."

"Exactly what I was hoping to hear. What's your name?"

"Ed."

Jack looped his arm around Ed's shoulders. "Ed, I need your help rather badly."

"Help with what?" Ed ducked out of Jack's man-hug, his voice betraying his reluctance.

"Take off your uniform."

Ed held up his hands and took a step backward. "Dude, I ain't no freakie-deakie. Just sign for the envelope, and I'll be on my way."

Jack looked over his shoulder. The crowd outside was growing both in size and in media presence. "I don't have time to explain." He pulled out his wallet. "How much?"

Ed looked at Jack from beneath furrowed brows. "You want to buy my uniform?"

"How much?" Jack began counting off bills. "One hundred? Two hundred?"

"I can't sell you my uniform."

"Five hundred," Jack cut in.

Ed's head snapped up, a smile congealing on his lips. "A thousand."

"That's extortion," Jack countered.

"I'll need to buy a suit for the unemployment line."

Jack nodded. "Ok then. How about five hundred and a job in the mail room? A nice 9-to-5 job with no package delivery weirdness."

"Weirdness like this?"

Jack shrugged. "How about it?"

"Five hundred, and I run the mailroom."

"Deal." Jack handed him the cash.

Rashesh leaned over. "What about Walter?"

"Walter is officially promoted," Jack replied.

"To what?"

Again, Jack shrugged. "You're COO, Rash, you'll figure out something." He turned his attention back to Ed. "Done. Take off your pants." Jack began to unbuckle his belt.

"Whoa, buddy." Ed backed away. "I don't mind watchin' a strip show, but I don't want to be in one."

Jack pointed. "Closet is over there. Light switch to the left inside."

Ed walked over and put his hand on the doorknob. "No peeking."

Jack laughed. "Not even at gun point."

Chapter Eighteen

On the ride home rain started falling, making Kinley's mood even gloomier. Again, she trusted the wrong guy. She thought she had to make the first move because Jack had become accustomed to being invisible. She thought the only way he would know how attractive he really was both inside and out would be if she showed him. And she thought the only way she would know she had moved from the past hurt and was ready to commit to someone would be if she showed herself.

Only, her worst fear had been realized. She made the same humiliating mistake as she had before. Liars didn't care for anyone but themselves.

She felt incredibly stupid. Jack had been a fabulous actor—playing the nerd, hiding out in her life, and going back to the world of business and money when it suited him. How could she have been so wrong? Better question—would she ever get it right?

Suddenly, she felt as though a hand grabbed her heart and squeezed. Oh my God. That's why he didn't want them to get too close. He didn't want to make any mistakes. Didn't want any lingering reminders of the chase, or of accidental commitments, or of promises made to anyone who might lay claim to his gaming legacy.

She pulled into her driveway feeling tears form in her eyes. Frustration slugged through her pulse. The first betrayal had taken a lot out of her; this one had taken more. Maybe it had taken the rest of what she could ever give someone else. She had managed to crawl out of the hole the first one made in her heart. She'd crawl her way out of this one, too, though she suspected recovering would take longer.

Anger grew and swallowed everything else inside her. She couldn't tell if the anger resulted from her own doing or from what Jack had done to her, and she didn't care. She'd use the pain, and steel her heart.

She'd be okay.

****

A few hours later, Jack stared at Kinley's front door, hesitating. He rolled his shoulders, the navy fabric of the delivery uniform not giving an inch of space. He deserved the discomfort, he reasoned. His life was in shambles, maybe unfixable, so why shouldn't everything he touched or touched him feel awful.

He used to love to find his way through impossible situations, loved to work around problems and issues, and find solutions. But those situations existed in the virtual worlds he created, and the problems, those of incomplete threads and fractured bits and bytes. This problem was real, and involved flesh and blood and heartache.

He kept remembering how he and Kinley had gotten so close. He marveled how, for him, things moved from the kind of love you have when you throw your arm around the shoulder of a friend, to the kind of love that could mean forever and family.

If only he'd been truthful. But he had been such a coward knowing the only way a frog ever got to kiss a princess was to trick her into doing it. He hadn't meant to trick Kinley, but in his selfish need to be with her, he simply didn't tell her everything he should have.

For a while, his actions didn't feel like he was lying. He'd have done anything to stay close. Anything. Even hide the part of him that brought them together. Because of his cowardice, he had hurt her, and he had no idea if he could ever make things right.

He edged closer to her door, his heart hammering in his chest like a love-sick school boy. *No good.* He started to leave but only took two steps. For the love of Pete, what was he thinking? He had no choice. For her sake, and for the sake of his own sanity, he had to face her and go through with his plan. Maybe the frog in him would never really turn into a prince, but he knew the princess deserved an explanation of why not.

He curled his fingers into a fist, knocked, and waited. He heard her footsteps first approach the door and then heard her voice.

"Who is it?"

"Package delivery."

"I didn't order anything. Are you sure?"

"Yes, ma'am. Says so right here."

****

Kinley looked through the security viewer in her door. The label on the box he held up carried her name. She stepped back. "Leave it."

"Can't. Needs a signature."

She needed to get rid of this guy so she could get back to dealing with accepting that the first man she decided to trust after her ex-fiancé ripped out her heart had been leading a double life.

"Just a minute." She grabbed a pen from the table and ripped open the front door. "Where do I sign?"

But the delivery man said nothing. He just stood here holding the package in front of his face.

She waited, contemplating what to do next before blowing out a short breath of air in frustration. "Where do I sign?' she asked slowly, spacing out each word.

Jack slowly lowered the package he had been holding. "Kinley."

Her breath caught. It took every ounce of strength she could summon to speak. "Go away." She was in no mood for Jack. Physically and emotionally, she was a mess. Her stomach churned from too much anxiety, her head pounded from trying to figure out why he'd deceived her, and her nerves pulsed from the knife sharp feeling of dejection that refused to lighten. She attempted to slam the door in his face but he dropped the package and grabbed the door near the lock with both hands, holding fast when she tried to pull it shut.

"Kinley, please," he pleaded.

"Move your hands or lose your fingers," she demanded. The tug of war continued for a few minutes before she gave up. She cocked her hip. "What?" She hoped her voice sounded clipped because her throat was closing with a combination of anger and misery, and she seriously doubted she could say anything more.

"We need to talk."

A thin thread of emotion vibrated through her, and a fleeting thought suggested she listen to what he had to say. She tried to focus on it, but found herself too angry, too humiliated to hang onto anything rational. "No, we don't," she insisted.

"I'll talk then. Just please listen."

She saw his Adam's apple quiver when he swallowed hard.

"I owe you an explanation," he offered.

"And then in your flow-charted, game-playing world, you win?" she countered. "Not this time." In his body language, she could see his agitation rise, see disturbance in his eyes. She felt some control return. Like in one of his video games, he had failed the level, game over, and seeing that made her feel a little better. She clenched both hands and felt the bite of her fingernails on her palm. "How long did you plan this?" Swallowing hard, she forced ice into her voice.

He shook his head. "Nothing was planned."

"Everything you do is planned. It's how your linear world exists. Forward in an orderly pattern with no deviation from the course you charted."

"Not true. I didn't plan anything."

"You designed an alter ego of a trouble-shooting techie when, in fact, you owned the damn company."

"I can explain."

"No, you can't," she said quickly. "You used your position to meet techno-challenged women and become their hero when you saved them from data collapse."

He hesitated. Then it was too late.

"No denials?" Her tone moved to hard-edged grate. "Good thing I caught myself before I completely fell for the forlorn nerd persona."

"It's not a persona, Kinley."

She swept her hand in the air. "You're still pretending. Look at you. Now you're in package delivery."

"Would you have opened the door for me?"

"Maybe, if you had bothered to tell me truth some time during the last two years."

"Kinley, the truth is my life started changing the

day I came to fix your brother's gaming system. I had come to the conclusion I'd probably never have the life or family I dreamed of having, but after meeting you, I thought, maybe, just maybe, I was wrong."

She felt her head pound as the tension between them grew. "I never gave you that impression."

"No, you didn't. What you did was make me feel like I wasn't just a part of the furniture. You can't imagine how much that meant."

"I wasn't doing you a favor. I liked you. Right from the start. And now I find out I was the fool. Betrayal hurts, Jack."

"I know about hurt, Kinley," he whispered. "I lived it most of my life."

"And now you want to get even with the entire female race one woman at time? I thought we had something between us, but—" She stopped, her heart thudding, her blood feeling like ice water in her veins. The realization of how much work he had put into constructing his alter ego like a character in one of his video game systems stung her like a hard slap to the face. He had thought of everything, right down to the potential consequences. "That's why you stopped last night," she whispered. "You wanted no mistakes to complicate your life."

"Kinley, no. That's not true."

She felt the heat of humiliation rise on her chest. "And I fell for it."

He reached out but she stepped back. "You misunderstood."

She raised her hand. "I didn't misunderstand anything. What I did was let down my guard and trusted a man who didn't care enough to tell me the truth." She lifted her chin in what she hoped look like a deliberate act of defiance. "Look, I can't do this any longer, Jack. Please. Take your hand off the door."

Her words were met with total silence until, after a long pause, he said, "I'll go. But I'm not giving up."

Her heart breaking, she watched him leave. She wanted to believe him, but twice bitten, she couldn't risk it. This betrayal had reopened the old wound.

But the thought of his warm brown eyes crept into her mind, along with the memory of how his lips curved into a smile she could never resist. He had pretended he was someone he wasn't, yet every thought that entered her mind now was of his kindness, and the way he had always wanted nothing more than to make her laugh.

She stared at her reflection in the hall mirror, her perfect reflection, and began to reconsider her actions. Maybe he had been afraid to tell her the truth about himself because of insecurity. Maybe she should grab onto what he offered, and listen to what he had to say. She thought about the intensity that sizzled when their gazes met, the warmth that grew when he said something funny, and the sheer enjoyment they felt when they were together. Suddenly, she missed him desperately. The hurt of betrayal rose inside her chest, and her mind shifted back.

But what about trust? No relationship could exist without it.

Chapter Nineteen

The driving ringtone of *Whatever Makes You Feel Like a Rock* Star by Kenny Chesney woke Kinley the following morning. Mike's ringtone. She thought about not answering, but knew her brother would keep calling until she did. With a groan, she reached for her cell.

"Sis, don't hang up!"

"Why would I?"

"Because I want to talk about Jack."

Her grip tightened. "Bye, Mike."

"Stop!"

"Why?" She brushed at the hair on her cheek.

"Because you are being ridiculous."

She left out a long breath of air. "You knew, didn't you?"

"Not until a little while ago."

Kinley felt the heat of humiliation climb up her neck and sting her cheeks. "Why didn't you tell me?" She could hear Mike stammer. "Did he bribe you to keep quiet with the offer of money?"

"No."

"A job?"

"No!"

Mike's denial was louder and more resolute. "Then why?"

"Because I kinda understood where he was coming from."

"Did he put you up to this, and tell you to say that?"

"No,"

"Don't lie," she countered. "I am tired of being lied to."

Mike paused. "Okay. He did ask me to call you."

"And so you have." Then she hung up.

Seconds later, again, Kenny Chesney blared. Mike was just as stubborn as she was. Family trait. She'd be listening to that ringtone until Mike made his point. "What did he promise you?" she asked him when she answered.

"He didn't promise anything."

"Then why are you taking his side."

"I'm not taking sides. I just think you should listen. Haven't you ever had your confidence shot to hell?"

"Everyone has confidence issues in the life at one time or another," Kinley replied, her tone clipped.

"Issues because of the way you looked?"

"Oh for Pete's sake," Kinley said with a long rush of air. "We're not in high school any longer, Mike."

"I am, and I've done crummy stuff to kids because of how they looked. Maybe I made fun of a dude with pimples, or a chick bigger than some of the hot babes in my class but still trying to wear those bangin' booty shorts. I'm not proud of myself, especially now, but I did it," Mike admitted.

Her brow furrowed. "Those are pretty awful things to do, Mike."

"I know that now. I never realized what a jerk I was, or how something like cruel words stay with a person until I saw what happened to Jack after the accident, and realized how unsure he is about

213

everything because of it."

"Jack will be fine. He looks like a GQ model and, apparently, is filthy rich. He should have no more problems in any area."

"Ya think? Yeah, he got it all now, and now that he does, how does he figure out who wants what?"

In no mood for riddles, Kinley snapped back in a sarcastic tone, "Who wants what *what*?"

"His money, his body, or him? Sure, he's a good-looking dude with a whole lot of Benjamins, but things don't change, sis. The cheerleader wants to be seen with the hot-shot quarterback because he's good eye candy and can get her places. Fast forward a few years. Now the hot babe ex-cheerleader wants a Ferrari and unlimited credit on a gold American Express card, and she's looking for a rich guy who'll put a ring on her finger so she can get everything she wants. The media served up Jack as one of those rich, available guys on a silver platter for all the chicks like that ex-cheerleader. Now it's a no-brainer for the dating black widows, because along with the bucks, the guy in question looks like a movie star instead of a geek."

Stunned, Kinley did not know how to react. Her teenaged brother suddenly sounded like the teacher, making her feel like the student. Conflicting thoughts of head and heart assailed her. Some days she was ready for a confrontation with her brother, and they did have a track record of loving each other rather loudly at times, but today was not one of those days. Today, she wanted to sit on a chair, cover herself with an afghan, and grasp the heavy sense of loss that engulfed her. "I'm hanging up, Mike."

"After you do, think about what I said," Mike's

fading voice pleaded.

She took the phone from her ear and punched it off. "Think about it," she repeated. "Like I have a choice."

****

Jack looked out his office window at the waning media frenzy in the street below. The news trucks were leaving. He had given the news crews what they wanted. Snippets of his interview already aired on a few channels. He hoped those reading, watching, or listening would realize all that happened was simply because he went out for Chinese, and had an automobile accident. A bad accident. Plain and simple. No covert planning to manipulate stock prices. No tricking the stock holders. He simply was in the wrong place at the wrong time.

Right after the accident, with the amount of pain killers in his system, he had been only on the fringes of what was happening. He remembered agreeing with the doctors when they told him they would have to reconstruct his face. He figured on a few tweaks— straighten the nose that had been broken when that kid from the wrestling team shoved him into a locker back in the tenth grade, maybe get rid of those hereditary saggy eyelids. The doctors may have asked him if he wanted a few others changes to his face, but he couldn't be sure. In and out of a mind-emptying sleep and waking moments filled with mind-blowing pain, he'd just let them do their jobs.

He didn't ask for an Adonis face, nor did he expect to get a better body from simply doing the physical therapy he needed to heal. But both happened, and he would have to find a way to function in his new skin. The surgeries might have been a success, but the failure to handle the result afterward was his self-made fiasco. Who would have guessed modern medicine could have ended up a modern curse?

He heard his office door open and turned with the sound.

Mike came in, shaking his head. "Dude, you're screwed."

"You have a knack of stating the obvious." Jack slipped into his desk chair, picked up the phone, and dialed.

"If you're trying to get my sister, she won't answer."

"I know." He punched the speaker button, the sound of Kinley's telephone ringing filling the room. After the fifth peal, he hung up and dialed again.

Mike tossed his head. "She's turned off her voicemail. If you keep calling, listening to her voice mail message will get boring after a while."

"She may pick up."

"No, she won't."

"She will," Jack insisted.

"She doesn't have to check the number on the caller ID to know it's you calling her. I showed her how to download ringtones, and she gave me and you each one to match our personalities. Mine's *Rock Star*."

"Great." Jack frowned. "What's mine? *Wanted Dead or Alive*?"

Mike laughed and gave him a thumbs-up sign. "Good one."

"What else did you show her how to do?"

"Nothing. Teaching her ringtones took an hour, and I had to restore the settings a few more times. Even after two years with you, she still doesn't speak geek."

Jack felt both wounded and relieved. Reminding him of the time he spent with Kinley teaching her not to destroy her computer hurt, but hope flourished in the fact she never quite got the technical stuff, and she still may need him someday.

If she ever decided to speak to him again.

If she got over what he did to her.

If she didn't take a computer course so she'd never have to see him.

Too many ifs. The situation seemed hopeless.

"When she gets tired of hearing your ringtone, she'll try to block your call, you know," Mike continued.

Jack shifted to analytical mode. "And when she does, chances are she'll wipe out something on the phone and—" He stopped speaking and stared at Mike for a full minute. "You're getting a raise."

"Why?" Mike's confused eyes stared back.

"Because you are a genius and just solved my problem."

Mike narrowed his gaze. "I didn't do anything."

"Then you're inspiring." Jack turned to his laptop and began punching keys. "Don't go anywhere. I may need you."

"What are you doing?" Mike asked, looking over Jack's shoulder.

Jack felt himself smile for the first time in a few days. "Hacking."

Chapter Twenty

In her home office, Kinley realized she had been staring at a chart keyed up on her laptop screen for the past hour. After she hung up on her brother, she thought if she immersed herself in work, she could get away from all the conflicting feelings. Then maybe, just maybe, a solution could seep into her tangled brain. She had been dead wrong.

She shook her head slowly, thinking over everything Jack said since the day they met, and remembering everything they'd done together. Torn between anger and understanding, she had no idea which emotion would eventually win.

She started to enter into the database when a red bar appeared on the laptop screen followed by an Alert Message:

Threat   found—Object— c:\users\Appdata\local\low\content.IES\Osmahelfnk\eic ar[4].com

Threat: Eicar test file—Comment—event occurred on a new file created: C\program Files\explore.exe.

"Not now!" she shouted. The report was due in the morning. Of course, she hadn't bothered to save it, or email the file to work, or back up the program on a flash drive, or the hard drive the last time she worked on the presentation.

Scrambling, she dumped her purse on the desk and

grabbed her cell, dialing and praying at the same time. She got Mike's voicemail. Not good. In desperation, she hit the escape key on the keyboard. Nothing happened. She punched it again and again with the same result. The angry pulsating error message kept flashing across her laptop screen, telling her she was totally screwed.

She snapped shut the laptop. She knew what she had to do.

****

Jack stood with his back to the door, looking out his office window. The activity seemed to be all he did lately. He rubbed a thumb over the ache in his head. He considered himself a smart man with access to a cajillion resources on an equal number of subjects. Why, then, didn't he have the foresight to find a Dating for Dummies book, a How to Talk to a Lady Blog, or an instruction manual on women complete with flow charts somewhere on the internet? Maybe if he had, he wouldn't have lost the woman he loved, the only woman he would ever love, before they ever dated.

His office was as quiet as a mausoleum, so he had no trouble hearing the door open, or honing in on the familiar voice started almost at the same time. "Jack, the Securities and Exchange want to come in and—"

"Rash, not now." Jack held up a hand.

Rashesh let out an exasperated sigh, the same kind of sigh Jack heard every time he didn't want to deal with something as quickly as Rashesh did.

"If not now, when?" Rashesh asked.

Jack turned. "You handle the SEC. I'm taking some time off to figure out what to do about the rest of my life now that I have totally smashed it against a brick wall." He walked to his desk and retrieved his cell phone.

"How long will you be gone?"

Jack shrugged. "A week, maybe a month."

"When did you decide that?"

"A minute ago."

"And what about Gaming?"

Jack tucked the phone into his inside jacket pocket. "You can run it. I trust you."

"You can't just up and leave. The company is at a crucial juncture. You have some decisions to make." Rashesh blocked the way when Jack started for the door. He put his hand on Jack's chest. "You can't let a little spat with Kinley affect the future of this company."

Jack looked at the hand on his chest. "We didn't have a little spat. We had an argument that was like the end of the world. My world. I have to get away for a while. I need to think. Since the accident, nothing has been the same. I'm trapped underneath this strange face and I can't get anyone to realize—" *Nothing's changed just because I, an insecure dork, went out for Chinese food and got a makeover instead.*

"Realize what?" Rashesh cocked his head, waiting for an answer.

Jack shrugged. "People don't change just because he or she puts on better-looking clothes."

"No one is making you change but you," Rashesh said. "I don't care what you look like. No one who buys your games cares about what you look like. Only the media cares. Most of us just want you to be the brilliant computer business mogul you are and always were. Don't let the press or anyone change you."

Jack forced a grin, although it took a Herculean effort to do so. "That's not the way of the world, Rash."

"Then make it so. You made this company from a garage business. It has the potential to be one of the best. All the guys who were ever kicked in the teeth for how they looked or what they wore are holding their collective breaths waiting to see what will happen next." Rashesh lowered his hand. "Don't let them down."

Jack started to respond when the door to his office flew open and crashed against the walnut bookcase. He turned toward the sound and saw Kinley outlined by the doorframe with a laptop in her hands. She took two steps inside, looked at Rashesh and glared. "You. Out!" Then she walked to Jack and hit him in the stomach with the laptop. "You. Stay."

After the door closed, Kinley dropped the laptop on Jack's desk. "Fix it."

Jack didn't move.

"Don't think I'm here for anything more than repairing my computer either," she continued. "I need a file trapped in there."

Jack still didn't move.

"I know you had something to do with my computer crashing. Fix it so I can get out of here."

"I know you're angry with me," Jack finally ventured.

"Very." She crossed her arms over her chest. "Now sit and fix what is wrong so I can finish what I started."

"That's exactly what I want to do, too," Jack said as he gazed at her beautiful-when-angry face.

"I'm still talking about the computer."

Jack captured her gaze with his. "I'm not. I know

I've made a few bad decisions when it came to you."

"Like doing whatever you did to make my laptop blink like a pinball machine gone tilt?"

"You're right, Kinley. I sent you a virus." He pulled out his desk chair and sat, remotely fixing her computer with a few keystrokes. "There. All done."

"Why?" She knew why, but she wanted him to tell her. He needed to start talking. Not about bits and bytes and computer code, but about how he felt. If the small ghost of chance for them she still held onto inside her heart despite her anger would ever become real, she needed him to talk to her now.

He stayed silent for a long while before saying, "Because I needed to see you, and I didn't think I had any chance unless you needed me when your computer crashed."

"I *knew* it." Kinley threw up her hands, staying a careful distance away. "You're still using tricks, still hiding behind a veneer. Maybe it's hopeless."

Jack stood and walked to her. "If it's so hopeless, why did you come?"

She lifted her chin. "Because I deserve to know why you lied to me for two years, and I deserve to hear it from you. In person. Not by email or text message. Face to face, so I can look in your eyes and decide if you are still lying." She felt her own eyes begin to fill. "Damn you, Jack. Can't you see? I've tried to tell you that you are special. You help everyone, care about people, and you worry about how your decisions will affect others. You were that man before the plastic surgeons changed the way you look. Or at least I thought so. But now, I found out you were keeping a secret, one that affects me...affects us. And I heard it from a news reporter and not you." She looked at him, refusing to let the tears flow. "I thought I knew you. I let myself feel safe with you, and let down my guard. Then you ripped that all away."

Jack blew out a long breath. "Maybe I don't know who I am either," he admitted hoarsely.

Not wanting Jack to see her cry, she bit her lip and looked away. "A man I cared very much for went out for take-out one night after standing me up for dinner because he was wrapped up in a computer game. Maybe he was overweight and ordinary in looks, but those things didn't matter. He stood by me, helped me in all aspects of my life. He was kind, had a huge heart, was funny with a unique perspective on everything that makes me laugh."

"Stop, Kinley," he said, feeling the heat of embarrassment climb his neck to settle on his face.

"No. I need to finish. You refused to understand on your own, and now I know why. A big-time business mogul doesn't need someone like me in his life. You already had most of everything you ever wanted. The accident gave you the rest."

He started to move toward her but she held up a hand. He backed away. "Kinley, please. I don't want it to be like this between us. Believe me."

She felt an ache start in her heart, mirrored soon with one throbbing in her temples. "Believe you? How? Why?"

He shook his head. "I don't know." He looked down at the floor.

She heard him take a deep breath before looking back up.

"I could tell you I'm sorry, but I don't think

apologies will be enough."

"It wouldn't. You hurt me, Jack. By deceiving me as you did, you put me in the same category with all the gold diggers out there you thought would only fall for you because you had money. Perhaps you didn't say it with words, but you certainly underlined it with your actions."

"That's not why I didn't tell you." He shook his head and then swallowed hard. "I didn't tell you about the company because of who I was. I didn't tell you because of who you were."

Kinley felt her brow furrow with the confusion she felt. "What kind of person do you think I am if you felt you had to lie?" No tears were falling, but she could feel them welling in her eyes.

"I know I hurt you," Jack began. "But that was never the plan. When I fixed your computer that day two years ago, everything changed for me. The way you talked to me, the way you were interested in what I did, made me feel like someone and not just a piece of furniture. I was over the moon. After a few months, each time I started to tell you about the company and how I felt about you, the old fears and insecurities came back and I couldn't do it. I didn't want things to change between us."

He looked down again and then quickly back up. "I wanted to tell you everything. And I should have. The reason I didn't tell you wasn't because I didn't trust you. I didn't trust me to be the man you deserved. Can you ever forgive me for the mess I made?"

He tried to reach for her but she took a step back. "I fell in love with you over those two years. I wanted to tell you the night you had the accident. I'm sure I loved you from the very first second I saw you," he admitted. Maybe she wasn't ready to let him hold her just yet, but she didn't move when he started to take some slow steps forward.

"You told me you loved me at the hospital," he continued. "But I wasn't sure what kind of love you were admitting. Was it the kind of love I dreamed about, or the love for a someone you almost lost in a horrific car crash? I knew you loved me as a friend. I cherished that. I resigned myself to accept that if I couldn't have you as a lover or a wife, then I settle for the friendship. I dared not hope for more. We were such opposites."

"Are you saying you thought you would bore me because you considered yourself a techno-weed?" Kinley saw his expression cloud. "And if that's so, you better not come any closer because I will smack you."

But he had already come close enough to brush a lock of hair from her brow, close enough to cup her cheek and run a thumb lovingly over her lower lip. Close enough for her to kiss him. And she would do just that once she finished saying what she had to say.

"Ok, you've changed, and I have to get used to the new you. Okay, you did a little relationship dance, but I can understand why." She saw his eyes brighten for the first time since she walked into his office.

"You do?"

She nodded slowly. "Mike pulled the little-brother-done-wrong card from up his sleeve in an admission about the way he used to think about and treat other kids. He admitted that until your accident and transformation that came with it, he never realized how much words could hurt and how long the hurt could remain."

"Kind of like you and the guy who broke your heart? After I heard your experience, I felt just like him."

She sighed. "You're nothing like Mark, so don't think that. Ever." She looked into his beautiful eyes and thought she could see his soul, a soul so pure it took her breath away. "That night, I thought I lost you," she whispered. "My heart hurt with the thought I might not ever tell you how I felt." She smiled. "You saw me at my best and my worst and never judged me. You were my friend, and then became something so much more. No man ever came close to understanding me the way you did. I told you I loved you—"

"Only in the hospital after the accident."

"I would have told you at dinner," she admitted, then smiled. "But Dakota had a mission that took a little longer than planned, and you know the rest. In the hospital, when I saw you looking all mummy-like, I was so afraid. I didn't want the first time I said those words to be misconstrued, but I needed to say them, to tell you I loved you. I didn't know if you even heard me."

His gaze darkened, and Jack nodded. "I heard you."

She sighed. "When the bandages came off, you looked amazing. I knew from that moment on you would never again blend into the background. Women would notice you, Jack, and you deserved the chance to notice them back."

"I don't care about other women."

"How could you know?" She shook her head. "You told me you never dated much, and most women never gave you a second look. Now, things were about to change. Women would hit on you. Maybe you'd come to like the attention. Shouldn't you get the chance to have what every other guy has—the thrill of the chase?"

The promise of a smile curved his mouth. "I had a thrill like that for the last two years."

"Damn you, Jack," she said, seeing him through tears now. "Don't you understand? You look different. You will be different. From now on, women will be all over you, and you deserve to finally experience all the attention you never had all your life. You can't know what or who you want because you really never tested the dating waters." Her voice broke. "Maybe the woman of your dreams is still out there."

He shook his head. "Nice of you to offer to share, but I have to pass. I already found the woman of my dreams. I don't want any other woman but you. If you forgive me for putting off telling you about Gaming, I promise I will never hold back anything again."

Kinley sighed and bit down on her lip. "Trust is so important in a relationship. I didn't trust myself to take a leap of faith, and neither did you. So what does that say about the two of us? If it tells us anything, maybe we are all wrong about something more to our friendship."

"Or we were both afraid."

"Fear can only be overcome by trust," she whispered over the lump in her throat.

"So we learn to trust all over again together. The only thing you have to believe right here and right now is I'm not a man who will manipulate people to get what he wants. I am only a scared coward. Think back about the way we got to this moment. Sure, we went in a few circles and took some detours, but we did get here. That has to mean something. I truly believe we can work anything out if you can believe it, too."

"I want to," Kinley confessed. "Really want to."

"Then let me prove it."

"How?" A flutter centered in her stomach.

"Close your eyes."

She did.

"What do you see?'

"Nothing."

"Good. Who am I?"

Her eyes popped back open.

"No peeking," he said.

When she closed her eyes, she felt him kiss each eyelid to be sure they were shut tight."Who am I Kinley?" he asked again.

His voice sounded like seriousness coated in warm honey "Jack Reeves, a business giant with a lot of money, not a computer fixer. You're a man who has a new face and can have a new start because of a car accident."

"And how do you know?"

"From the media hype."

"Now keep your eyes closed. What do you know about me just by the sound of my voice? Don't tell me what's on or in the news. Tell me what you know from the last two years we spent together by listening to my voice. Just from my voice. Tell me what you know about that man."

She took a deep breath. "You're Jack Reeves, the most amazing man I have ever met. You're different than other men. You care. Really care. Not just about people, but about how your actions and decisions affect others. Maybe you care too much, so you ignore what you need for yourself. You make sure things are perfect for everyone else, even if it means you have to lose a little. That's just the way you are—everyone else first, you when you get to it. But I love that."

"Now open your eyes," he told her.

When she did, she felt the tension leave her body. Jack had put on his old glasses, the ones held together with electrical tape. A flood of happy memories wrapped her in warmth, and she felt tears start a trail down her cheek. How foolish was she to think Jack would ever change on the inside just because he had been forced to accept a change on the outside. Maybe he couldn't control what the doctors did to save his life, but inside, he would always be Jack Reeves. The same Jack Reeves she met the day she tried to kill her computer. The same Jack Reeves who had her heart.

"You don't need those any longer." She reached out and removed the glasses.

He took his glasses from her hand and put them on the desk. "I'll keep them anyway. They remind me of the old days."

She reached up and traced his lips. "I love you no matter what you look like." The smile she loved slowly curved his mouth.

He slipped an arm around her waist, cocked his head, and brought his face to within a heartbeat of hers. Breathing in the scent of Kinley. "And I love you no matter what you look like." He saw confusion run wild in her eyes.

"I know I'm not Hollywood beautiful, but I don't remember turning anyone to stone lately."

Jack kissed the tip of her nose. "Medusa, you're definitely not. Want me to explain?"

She smiled. "Please. By all means."

"When I first met you, I could barely look you in the eye. You stole my breath. But I knew the drill, so I told myself she's out of your league, Reeves. Fix the computer and get out. Then you talked to me. Not down to me but *to* me, and I felt special. Only an impulse, a last second, take-the-shot moment, made me ask for your phone number. I never thought you would actually give it to me. Not in a million years. Not in a hundred million years. But you did." He stared into her beautiful eyes. "And I swear I heard angels singing."

Slowly, she shook her head. One hand wrapped around his neck and then the other. "Reeves, when will you listen? Maybe you think you don't deserve to be happy, and think you should hold back, but you are wrong. If you kiss me right now, I can show you what I mean."

Since she asked, he complied. And since he knew this time he didn't have to worry about a slap or a misunderstanding, he took his time, kissing her long, deep, and hard. In his kiss was a lifetime of dreams, and hopes of cuddling on a back porch swing, and making wild passionate love on the living room floor. He wanted to confess more with this kiss, but he had to come up for air.

"Wow," she whispered breathlessly when he broke contact with her lips. "See what I mean?"

What he saw was someone he intended to spend the rest of his life making happy because in two short years, she had made him happier than he ever thought possible."I see a whole lot of things more clearly now," he admitted. "Another thing I see is someone I still owe dinner. How about we finally get that Chinese?"

Kinley frowned and shook her head. "I don't think I want take-out ever again."

"I wasn't thinking take out. How about dinner at Tim's Kitchen?"

"If the place is close. I am hungry," Kinley said. "I'd love an egg roll and fried rice about now."

Jack's smile broke wide. "The restaurant I have in mind isn't exactly close and doesn't exactly serve Chinese. More like Cantonese, and well worth the time it will take to get there."

"New York?"

"No, Hong Kong." He reacted to her wide-eyed expression. "I'm rich, remember?"

Epilogue

"He looks great up there, doesn't he?"

"He sure does." Kinley watched Jack acknowledge a question from the audience at the Q&A session set up the first afternoon of the Computer Electronics Expo on the conference floor of the Wynn Hotel in Las Vegas. "He's really come into his own lately."

"You've helped with that," Rashesh pointed out. "His confidence is through the roof since you two became a real couple. He did a great job convincing the SEC no one schemed to manipulate the stock's IPO. Once he was cleared, the stock traded at an all-time high. He saved a lot of jobs at the company and made a lot of people who believed in him a ton of money."

Kinley laughed. "That confidence was always inside him. He just needed some help getting it to the surface."

Jack had finished the last question and began making his way to them. His gaze never left hers except for the few seconds he acknowledged the CEX organizer. As soon as he was by Kinley's side, he slid his arm around her waist.

"Okay then," Rashesh said. "That speech was all you had for the rest of the night, and remember, three's a crowd. Besides, I hear a Black Jack table calling my name."

"Don't lose your entire expense account," Jack

called as Rashesh headed off.

Rashesh acknowledged with a wave.

Jack turned his full attention to Kinley. "Thanks for hanging around. I gave you my American Express. You could have gone shopping."

She handed it back. "I charged coffee and a bagel, but, still, the bill was ten dollars."

"It's Vegas. Everything costs more."

"Doesn't mean I have to run up a huge tab."

Jack pulled her closer. "Marry me, and I'll get you a card with your own name."

"Bribery doesn't work," Kinley said, leaning her head against his chest.

"Then marry me, and I promise I won't get you one. Just marry me. Here. Now. Before something else happens."

Expecting to hear him laugh off the comment, she remained quiet for a few moments. But then, so did he. And a shiver ran over her skin. "You're serious," she finally said.

"Very. There's a drive-through chapel on every block along the strip. Pick one. When we get home, we'll have a proper wedding."

Kinley tapped her forefinger on her chin. "You know, my friend Ali Archer got married here by an Elvis impersonator a few years ago. She said he was very good, and she's very happy."

"I don't need the minister to be good. All I need is happy and legal and your name and mine on a marriage license. Besides, I know from experience all great adventures start at Level One, and this appears to be it. So, what do you say? Shall we hit start and see what's in store?"

Kinley nodded, slowly at first and then more definitively. "I say lock and load, Dakota, because this adventure is one we're taking together, and it promises to be a hell of a ride."

A word about the author…

Born long ago in a place not so far away, Shenandoah, Pennsylvania, Kathye Quick has been writing since the Sisters in St. Casmir's Grammar School gave her ruled yellow paper and a number two pencil. She writes contemporary romances, romantic comedies, and historical romances, as well as urban fantasy.

She has been a member of New Jersey Romance Writers (President in 1992 and 2001), is a current member of Liberty States Fiction Writers, and Romance Writers of America. She is one of the founding members of Liberty States Fiction Writers, a multi-genre writers' organization dedicated to furthering the craft of writing and helping aspiring writers move on to publication.

Kathye originally wanted to be President of the United States or an organic chemist, but somehow life got in the way when she married right out of high school and had a set of twins two years later. The Presidency seemed out of reach, and night school to get her Ph.D. so she could create a new molecule that would ultimately result in the betterment of humankind seemed a little time-consuming while trying to raise twins, so she decided to write instead.

Kathye is married to her real-life hero Donald and has three grown sons all having adventures of their own. She is a die-hard New Jersey Devils fan and works for Somerset County government (as close as she could get to the White House).

www.kathrynquick.com